TRAIL OF THE
SPIRIT WARRIOR

TRAIL OF THE SPIRIT WARRIOR

Western Historical Fiction

Roger L. Haley

RAMBLE HOUSE

ISBN 13: 978-1-60543-531-2

ISBN 10: 1-60543-531-7

Cover Art: Gavin L. O'Keefe
Preparation: Fender Tucker

A word from the author

After joining Western Writers of America, and having conversations with other writers, editors, and publishers, I found that I had broken a cardinal rule in "*Kiamichi Trail*" . . . I left my readers hanging about the fate of Mourning Dove, Jonathon's Choctaw bride. After much discussion, it was determined that the best way to fix this was to do a rewrite of "*Kiamichi Trail*", remove it from the market, and write a much longer book that resolves the issue.

Thus was born "*Trail of the Spirit Warrior*". Herein, we get the beginning of Jonathon's tribulations, along with the tale of his time with the Texas Rangers and his continued search for his bride. This time, hopefully, I leave you with a sense of finality when the story ends.

My deepest gratitude to all who emailed me or left messages on my website about the pleasure you got from reading my story. Jon, Rip, Mourning Dove, and all of the other characters, are alive to me. I write about them as I believe they would have lived. For example: my original intent was for Jon to remain with the Rangers, but I soon realized that he was not the type of man who could ignore the plight of Mourning Dove. Because of the way I viewed him, I had to change the entire story. The reality that exists only in a writer's mind can be compelling; I had to be true to his values.

Other than the fictional characters, the people and places I write about do—or did—exist. The battle with the Comanche really happened, Fort Towson is really there, as is Fort Riley.

I sincerely hope you enjoy this book. Please let me know at www.rogerhaley.com, or rogerhaley@yahoo.com. Contacting the publisher will only slow down any communication. Many thanks to those who have given me the impetus to continue writing.

For Dave, Sandy (Honey Bear), and Marie
Friends are the family you choose!

Chapter 1

"SON, IT IS NOT IN A MAN to always understand the actions of our Maker. When your ma died, I ranted and railed at Him for weeks but finally come to accept that He had left me with a son who needed my care, and maybe He needed your ma more than I did."

The memory of my paw's words comforted me as I stood on that lonely knob over the mound of fresh turned earth and felt the whisper of the dying breeze ruffle my hair. Hat in hand, I watched it flow off down the valley, rustling through the grass as it dried the final dampness on my cheeks.

I never knew my mother, for she had died on my bornin', and that pile of fresh dirt held the remains of my paw. I was alone now. Fifteen years alive, and the last of my line.

I could still hear Paw's voice as he told me so many times, "Whatever comes our way, Son, we can handle it. With the Lord's blessin' and our own determination and courage, we'll see it through."

Well, he was gone now, and I wondered if I had the backbone that he'd tried so hard to instill in me. It looked like I had no choice but to find out, or lay down and die. He'd be mighty ashamed if I did that, so I reckoned I'd keep on tryin'.

My paw had not been an overly lovin' kind of man but had always shown me his gentler side. Oh, he had him a temper I reckon, but I'd only seen it once or twice and that was plenty enough. I knew I'd miss him somethin' terrible.

I took one last look down that meadow at the grass movin' slow, like timid waves crossing a lake of green, the half-set sun just bouncing bits of light off the tips. Then, all used up, I settled my battered old hat atop my mop of coal black hair and headed for the cabin. I had a heap of thinking ahead of me.

That tumble down cabin would be mighty lonesome with just me and ol' Rip there. Rip was a big, dirty yeller kinda dog who'd just come walkin' up to the cabin a few years back, one ear sorta chewed by some critter he'd tangled with. He reminded me some of a black dog I seen once, only Rip was bigger. I reckoned he'd run about a hundred and twenty pounds or more and I figured him for a mix of some kind.

With me bein' about twelve years old then, and with never a dog to call my own, I taken to him right off. That tore up ear just naturally led to the name "Rip". Now Paw had always been tolerant of me and Rip, but he wouldn't have had no truck with a dog in the cabin.

"Jon," he said on that day, "If you plan to let that ol' dog hang around, it's your responsibility to care for him and teach him. He ain't allowed inside, so you'll have to make him a spot in the lean-to. And, if he can't feed hisself, you'll have to provide for him."

"I swear, Paw. I'll make sure he's a good dog and has plenty to eat. Why, I'll bet he can help me catch rabbits and such!"

Smiling at my enthusiasm, Paw just said, "Don't make promises 'less you plan to keep 'em, Son. A man's got to keep his word."

"Yes Sir, I'll shore take good care of him. I promise." And I did. Sometimes it was tiresome, but most times me and Rip had a great time rangin' about the woods, swimmin' in the creeks, and generally bein' a boy and his dog.

Bein' as it was only Rip and me now, and I didn't want to be alone, I held open that door and invited him on in. He just kinda looked at me, sniffed a couple of times, and sashayed on over by the fireplace like he'd been doin' it all his life. He circled twice, and then settled down on the rug.

"Rip," I says to him, "Me and you got to study some on what we do now."

A fifteen year old boy and a big yeller dog, all alone, might have a time of it here in these hills, and I was sure wonderin' which way to jump as I took stock of our worldly goods.

First off, we had a leaky, leanin', wind blown cabin settin' on a rocky hillside where wouldn't nothing grow but rabbits, squirrels, and trees. Of these, there was plenty, and we had a small meadow and truck patch nearby.

Next, there was Paw's horse. He was a surefooted blue roan, kinda rangy, but he could travel all day and night on a handful of grass and the dew licked from a leaf. Paw's saddle weren't much, but better'n none, that's for sure.

I had my squirrel gun, Paw's long gun, and his Walker colt. It was a 44 caliber, and named for a Texas Ranger, Sam Walker, who'd helped Samuel Colt design it. My squirrel gun hadn't seen much use 'cause I was real handy at flinging rocks to get squirrels and rabbits, but Paw had taught me a lot about shootin' so I weren't too bad at it.

Anyway, these few things, a bait of flour and salt, some venison, my kit, and forty-four dollars in coin that Paw had put back for hard times just about summed up my wealth. Now we had to get on with stayin' alive.

~ ~ ~ ~ ~

It weren't unusual for Paw to leave me alone for a few days while he went about the hills and worked or traded for the necessaries that we couldn't hunt, catch, or grow for our own selves. This last time though, he'd been gone longer than usual and it got worrisome. Long about sundown on the thirteenth day his horse come home without him.

Now Paw had taught me not to be foolish and not to rush off into something I hadn't studied on. Bein' near dark, I reckoned on waitin' for morning to take up the back trail of that roan. Weren't no sense in trampin' around them woods in the dark, maybe messing up what sign there was, so I taken that horse to the lean-to and rubbed him down good. I fed him a bite of what corn I had, and me and Rip settled in.

Long before gray-up that next morning, me and Rip ate, packed my kit, and saddled up. Knowin' how he'd come up to home, picking up the roan's trail weren't hard. Being without a hand on his reins, he'd perambulated somewhat between, betwixt, and around trees and deadfalls. Not wanting to lose the trail, I went right back along his track, stopping once in awhile to just sit asaddle, study on things, and listen to the hills whisper. With ol' Rip roaming out around me, sometimes ahead, sometimes back, I wondered about Paw. He had to be hurt bad, or dead, or he would have come in with his horse.

Paw was a fair sized man, and strong. More'n once I'd seen him carry on with a hurt that would put many men abed. One time a mountain cat, not sensing Paw was nearby, had jumped his horse. Paw told me what happened.

"I knew the roan was skittish, but had no idea that cat was so close. I had dismounted and had my gun ready, but didn't see him before he jumped. Reckon he didn't see me either.

"I couldn't take a chance on shootin', not with him on the horse's back, so I hollered as loud as I could, hopin' to scare him. He looked at me, but didn't run, so I pulled my knife and jumped him, stabbin' him in the side. Well, I reckon that got his attention, 'cause he turned his claws on me. It was touch and go for a bit, but he finally lit out after I stuck him a few more times."

Paw had come on to the cabin then, all ragged and bloody, big gashes on his arms and shoulders, and weak from pain and bleedin'. Before he'd let me tend him though, we'd taken care of that horse. Only then did he allow me to wash and sew up his cuts.

One gash on his left shoulder, taken twenty-four stitches with sinew. Our only painkiller was a touch of whiskey, inside and out. Paw taken him a big slug, had me pour a little on his wounds, and then just sat there in that old hand built chair whilst I washed and stitched. He just looked into the fire and never a grunt nor groan come out of him. Yep, Paw was one hard man, but hard men had mishaps just like weak ones. If he was just bad hurt, Paw knowed I would come for him.

That roan had shore seen some country on his way home but his trail gradually led me eastward, deeper into the

Kiamichi Mountains. A traveling man had told us these were mighty pore mountains compared to some out in the far western lands, but they was all the mountains I knowed, and big enough at that.

It taken me two days to find Paw. He'd been shot through, and was dead as they left him layin'. The critters had been at him some, but I reckon the man smell had kept most of 'em at bay. I stepped down from that roan horse and studied sign before fetchin' Paw across his saddle and to his spot on that lonely knoll. He'd of wished to lie beside Ma I know, but she lay across the mountains to the east.

"Someday," he kept sayin', "we are going back there to visit her grave and let you meet your kin."—but we never got to it.

There'd been two of them, and they'd come up from behind like they was following him. Paw had turned to face 'em but his gun was still tied down when I found him, and he never was considered fast anyway. They hadn't robbed him, for he still had his gun and four dollars in his pockets, along with his folding knife. That seemed peculiar to me.

I wondered about his kit, but figured it had been brushed off somewhere along the trail and some critter had dragged it off for the food in it. I hadn't been lookin' for that kind of sign, and must of missed it. I did see where one of their horses had a kind of kicked out hoof on the back left. I could tell by the marks he made.

I knowed it weren't Indians what got him, 'cause of not being robbed, and the Indians hereabouts was mostly Choctaw or Chickasaw, with a few Cherokee or Seminoles, and they was mostly all tame. Why, there was even a school down north of Fort Towson for them. It was called the Spencer Academy, I think.

There could have been a few of the unsettled tribes around, but they didn't raid around here very often. Besides, these horses was shod. Nope, it was white men all right and the only white men I knowed of Paw ever havin' troubles with was them Wiggins folks further east in the mountains toward Fort Smith. One of 'em had tried to skin Paw in a deal and then, even dumber, tried to back him down with hard talk. Well, Paw whupped him right in front of some folks, told him he was a cheat, and rode off. There was some talk about him huntin' Paw, but it never come to nothin'. He tried to make out that Paw had suckered him, but word got around and folks allowed as he was just no account.

Now I had me a mind to saddle up, load them guns, and go have a talk with them Wigginses, but Paw's teaching come through. I reckoned I'd only get whupped, or killed, and that would have been a foolish thing. I had no proof, nor idea really, except that everybody else liked and respected Paw. Besides, I had some growin' to do, and things come to those that wait.

~ ~ ~ ~ ~

At fifteen, I was getting my growth and was already near six foot tall. Like I said, Paw was a big man, and he'd told me Ma was a fair sized woman, but shapely. Problem was, I'd been shootin' upwards faster than outwards. Oh, I was big boned and broad acrost the shoulders for my age, but lean and rawboned.

The years of trompin' those wild woods and runnin' with ol' Rip had toughened and leaned out my muscles so I didn't look my weight. Even so, I'd be no match for them Wiggins men, so me and Rip settled down to takin' care of business. Someday I'd find out about Paw.

We'd had a good corn patch that year, along with some taters, onions, and a few other vegetables. I tended that patch best I could, and hoped to get enough corn and such to get us through the winter. Of game there'd be plenty, and fish, but that horse would need some corn. Besides, a man can't live good on meat alone. If I was savin', I'd not need to ride down to Pine Ridge, where there was a little settlement, or Fort Towson, further south, to buy sugar, flour, salt and such.

One thing I had plenty of was powder and lead for my guns. Paw weren't one to run short. "As long as you got powder, you can get meat." He always said. "Buy ammo before food and you'll not go hungry. Spend your money wisely."

With forty-four dollars, I had a fair sum of spending money, but felt it wise to hold on to it as best I could. Come spring, I'd have a few pelts and hides, too. Like I said, being savin', we'd get by.

Well, me and Rip taken to the woods. I had a pair of brogans and, since Paw got 'em big, they still fit. I hadn't growed into his boots yet, but had a few pair of moccasins Paw had taught me to make. I liked them when huntin' or easing quiet like through the woods.

I'd learned well how to Injun up on things and once got almost close enough to touch a white tail afore it sensed me and ripped a hole through the brush. For the work at hand though, them brogans was just the ticket.

Besides tending my truck patch, I had to cut and haul wood, hunt and smoke meat and fish, cut some tall meadow grass for hay, chink gaps, and even sweep out that old cabin on occasion. What with cookin', eatin', and chores, the days just melted away like a late snowfall. Mild winters was common hereabouts but it could get pretty bad at times, and I had to be ready for it.

One morning I finally noticed the chill and took my old coat down from the loft where I used to sleep. When I put it on and reached for the door, that coat split right down the seam! It seems that size, like the weather, had snuck right up on me. I took that coat off and fetched Paw's. It were still a mite big, but come nearer fittin' than my own. I'd been wearing his shirts for some time now, but had thought little of it.

Along with chores, huntin', and such, I'd taken to walkin' out to the edge of the meadow and practicing with Paw's Walker Colt. For the longest, I didn't waste powder but just practiced getting it out of the holster and pointed in the general direction of what I pretended to shoot. Havin' a 9-inch barrel, it seemed almighty cumbersome. I had a thought of cuttin' off the barrel but seemed to have heard that would throw off the aim. One day I had another thought, cut down the holster!

Well, I didn't want to ruin Paw's holster, so I taken a piece of wild hog hide and I soaked it, cut it, and shaped it around that Colt. Using my awl and some rawhide string, I fixed it to a belt made from deer hide. I filed the sight plumb off, figurin' anything I had to sight on was to far off for a handgun anyway.

The front of my hand-made holster was cut plumb down to within about an inch of the bottom in front. The part up around the cylinder was split and shaped to hold that gun snug, if pushed down into it. If it was loosened first, that colt would slide right out the split by only liftin' it a few inches. I ran, jumped, and even rolled on the ground, but never lost it when it was snugged down. That holster was strange lookin' but, with practice, I could snake that six-shooter out pretty quick. It shore made fetchin' that hog-leg some easier.

The last traveling man to stop over at the cabin had stayed the night and broke fast with us. I'd laid up in my sleeping loft and listened to him and Paw yarn far into the night. We seldom got any visitors up here on the creek, so it was the thing to learn all one could of the country, politics, Indians, and other people when there was a chance. Many an educated and wise man traveled the lonely trails of this great land. That sleepless night, I learned of those far off mountains to the west, and the endless plains before them. Of desert country so dry a man was as good as dead if he didn't learn its secrets.

"There are cattle down in Texas with horns that'll reach from yore door all the way to the fireplace," he said. I was some skeptical of this, wonderin' how big them cows must be, but I believed most of what he said.

He also told Paw, "There's stories of men who make a practice of fast drawin' a hand gun. Some is said to be quick as a strikin' snake. I reckon a man will have to learn how to do it if he travels much, or else be on the lookout for any of them shootists."

This knowledge brought about my later practice. To most folks a gun was a tool, just like a hammer or a hoe. You took care of it and kept it handy for use when needed. Fast drawin' and such wasn't much heard of, but knowin' I might one day have the need, I went to studying on it.

One evenin', as was my wont, I stood to the edge of the meadow and picked out a piece of a stick about twenty feet away with a small knot in it. I drew, fired, and put up that long barrel Colt in what seemed the blink of an eye. The knot disappeared. Now I'd not make out to be a gunslinger, but figured I could hold my own if it ever became necessary. Practice, though, would not stop.

As I stood there quiet like and gazed out over the valley, I noted the color of the grass and the shortage of leaves on the trees. A single white flake drifted past my face from the lead colored sky and it hit me that winter was nigh, and I'd worked right through my birthday. I couldn't be sure, but I figured this was early November. I'd been born in mid September. Well, I'd done my best and now it was up to the man upstairs 'cause me and Rip was as ready as we'd get.

That was a shore lonesome winter. If it hadn't been for ol' Rip, who I talked to so much he taken to givin' me hard looks so's he could sleep, I'd of gone plumb crazy. I think Rip learned more of people, politics, and philosophy than he really wanted to know, but he, and Paw's books, kept me sane.

I was thankful that Paw had taught me my letters and helped me learn to read his books. With no spare time in the last few months, they were like new to me. One fellow, that Shakespeare, I hadn't liked before 'cause I just didn't understand his writing. Through that long winter, though, he became a friend and a comfort. Paw had said that many a man could quote whole pages from his books. It might be a cowhand or a banker, and it would often surprise you, the one's that knew of him, though it shouldn't have. Men in this country learned where they could and read what they had. Often, around a campfire, or wherever people met, men would exchange books, talk of them, and quote from others. Many a lonely cowhand carried a book or two in his bags. Sure, there were many ignorant and foolish types who had no desire to learn of anything they needn't know to make their way, but there were far more of the others who soaked up learnin' like a drought stricken prairie absorbed the rain.

I also read the Good Book, and put Paw's date of dyin' in there. I often looked at those pages, mostly written in Ma's hand, wonderin' about Ma and her kin. I'd never known them, but hoped to someday get back there and look 'em up.

~ ~ ~ ~ ~

Well, me, Rip, and that roan horse made it through the winter just fine. Towards the end we run short on flour, so I taken some corn and ground it with my mortar and pestle. This I mixed with a little flour, salt, and water, which made better fry bread than flour alone. I guess I hadn't learned it all, but I did learn not to feed beans and salt pork to a dog if you had to stay inside with him!

I hadn't gone soft that winter. On the better days, me and Rip still roamed the hills, fished some, toted wood and water, and hunted far from home. All of these labors had put some meat on me, and size. I topped out now at around six foot, and was packed solid. Taller and heavier than many a full growed man, I reckon I was uncommon large for my age. I was to stop growin' early, just as I begun, and finish up at an inch over six foot, with over two hundred pounds of pure muscle.

One day that spring, rubbin' an itch on my nose, I discovered face hair. Checkin' my reflection in the water bucket, I could even see dark shadows on my cheeks. I was becoming a man! Now I'd watched Paw with his straight razor, or skinnin' knife when camping, but he'd never had reason to teach me shavin'. That razor was some kinda sharp but, without too much bloodshed, I got the hang of it.

All this time, since I'd buried Paw, I hadn't seen a solitary white man, and only a coupla Choctaws, from a ways off. Since ol' Rip would now slip off to hunt alone, and get away from my jawin', I had it in me to head down south for a spell. I was needful of staples, and powder for both guns, and I really needed to hear a voice besides my own and see another face, even if an ugly one.

I had me that cash money, but I'd be takin' many rabbit pelts, a few beaver, and some deer hides I hadn't used to make moccasins or britches with. I figured to sell the squirrel gun, trade for what I could, and get me some boots, shirts, and socks. Paw's boots now fit me but chaffed somethin' awful since all my socks was wore out. I'd tried my hand at buckskin shirts without much luck. Britches was all I could do good, and some of them weren't pretty.

Come mornin', I give that roan a good bait of our last remaining corn and saddled up. Neither me nor Paw had ever named that horse, but called him 'the roan' or just 'Horse' when we spoke directly to him. I reckon he figured that was his name and it was as good as any. Anyways, I tightened his cinch and tied on my bedroll and kit afore mountin' up. He could carry me and pull the travois, but I'd also walk some, so as not to wear him too much.

I'd only been once with Paw down to Pine Ridge, and reckoned it was about two or three days south and west of our creek. Not knowin' the country beyond a kid's roamin' range, I decided to take my time and get the lay of the land. I weren't in no hurry since nothing was waitin' for me but that old cabin.

Rip was some excited to see me saddle up 'cause he knew that meant a trip. He kept runnin' to the meadow and back, but I taken my time ridin' out. I paused at the knoll and said a few words to Paw, hopin' him and Ma was together again, and rode on out of there.

The day was typical of early spring here in the mountains. A cool breeze sighed through the trees as the early mornin' sun peeked out from the hilltops, painting the sky with shades of blue and orange. It was pretty here in the backcountry come springtime. If a man weren't in to big a hurry to enjoy it, it surely rested the soul. Trees a greening and buddin' out, grass coming alive, and birds galore. Just crossin' that meadow, I seen cardinals, blue jays, robins, and plenty more. There was even a hummingbird that hovered alongside and inspected my yellow slicker before zippin' off.

This was country to make a man pause, and appreciate bein' alive, but it could be a hard country too. A man had to be alert and watchful. Indians weren't so much a problem anymore, but there were some within raidin' range that might take on a man alone. Some was said to have seen Comanche this far east, but of that I had no knowledge. You had to watch out for other things, too. Deadfalls, burrows, or just holes, might cripple a horse. A gimped horse wouldn't kill you in these woods, but a broke leg of your own just might. More than one pile of bleached, unburied bones littered these hills with no marker to tell the story of who and why. This was a place, too, where some bad men roamed.

We picked up a traveled trail a couple of days out. This, I reckoned, was a part of the trail I'd heard about, blazed by Robert Bean and Jesse Chisholm from Fort Towson to Fort Smith. I'd soon hit the road that was cut by the army in 1825, from Fort Gibson to Fort Towson. Pine Ridge lay along that route, somewhere south of that Spencer Academy. Like I said, I'd only been there once, and I was a kid then.

Chapter 2

THE NEXT DAY, I sat my saddle in a grove of pines, lookin' down on Pine Ridge. Weren't much stirrin' down there but a dog and a few chickens. Being close to noon, I reckoned folks was settin' up to eat.

There was one big cabin, built of logs, with a clapboard front and a sign that just read "store" in hand painted letters. Three smaller cabins was scattered around it with one of them havin' a long lean-to and corral. This figured to be the stable. Smoke in the distance told me of other cabins nearby. One end of the lean-to held what appeared to be a forge and anvil, so there might be a smithy here. Since the roan was needful of shoein', I hoped this was the case. There was three horses in the corral and a coupla Missouri mules.

After settin' and lookin' awhile, I told Rip not to whup that dog too bad, and we eased on down there. I hitched the roan in front of the store and, slapping the dust from my well-used hat, stepped inside.

Nobody was there, but a bell tinkled as the door opened. To my left was two barrels with a board acrost them and with jugs and glasses in back. This must pass for the bar. Further down that wall was a pot bellied stove with three old rockin' chairs pulled up. Past the stove was a rough-cut table and two hand-made benches just big enough to seat two. You'd have to pull the table out to sit by the wall.

A slight, gimpy old man come from the back as I took stock of the place. There was a big counter down the middle filled with all sorts of stuff. There was lanterns, pots, pans, traps, and such, and on top was rows of shirts, long underwear, bolt goods, and britches. There was even a few western style hats with round brims. The right wall was filled with more shelves, top to bottom, that held sacks of flour, sugar, salt, beans, and more. There was tins of peaches, tomatoes, and—well, altogether more food than I'd ever seen in one place.

"Howdy." The old man called from a counter near the back that held even more stuff! Rock candy, of which I'd had little, bullet molds, pistols, knives, and pocket watches— a treasure trove to a country boy like me. I didn't recollect all of this from our last visit here, probably 'cause my eyes had been glued to that candy.

"Howdy." I finally replied. I reckoned this was old Mr. Wesely who was said to have settled here long ago.

"You be wantin' a drink to settle the dust?" he asked.

Now my size might of throwed him some but in reality a boy my age, travelin' alone, could buy a drink if he had the want and the coin. Not bein' a drinkin' man, I just told him, "No thanks." Now Paw might take a nip now and again, or put a drop in his coffee on a cold night, and I had nothin' against a drink, but felt no need to spend money on it. Not many folks had much tolerance for drunkenness, though.

"But I surely would like somethin' to eat what I didn't cook. Reckon you got that?"

"Why shore," he says, "set down on that bench there and the missus will bring it. Ma, fetch my plate and bring a heapin' one for this young feller," he called to the back.

He pulled the table out and eased onto the bench near the wall. I took off my hat and occupied the other. Sarge wore the years on his face. He was tanned a dark brown, and had wispy gray hair covering his head. It was thicker over the ears and around the back, but gettin' mighty thin on top. You could tell he had once been bulky; it showed in the breadth of his shoulders, but age had thinned him. He had a pleasant look about him.

"Name's Sarge Wesely," he offered his hand, " Don't reckon I know you."

It actually took me a second to even recollect my own name. It'd been so long since I heard anything but 'Sonny', which was what Paw had mostly called me. Sarge must of wondered at the pause, and my slight grin, when I finally responded, "Stout, Sir. Jonathon Ryan Stout. The Ryan is from

22

my Ma's people back East. Folks mostly call me Jon, or Jonny."

"Jonathon Stout," he mused. "The Stout seems familiar, are you from up around the Kiamish?" He pronounced it like a lot of folks did.

"Yes Sir, my paw was Grayson Stout."

"Was? What happened to him?"

Before I could answer, a wide, smiling woman emerged from the back, bearing two heapin' platters of beans, venison steak, sliced onion, fried okra, and cornbread. Her black hair braided and streaked with gray, she appeared right friendly but said nothing.

Well, jawin' would just have to wait while I surrounded that platter of home cookin'. It was a feast to a man who'd et his own cookin' for so long, and had subsisted on fry bread and jerky on this trip. Before we'd even finished, she came back out with two big quarters of fresh baked apple pie and refilled our coffee mugs. That broad, sweet-faced woman was gettin' prettier by the minute! I wondered how old Sarge stayed so skinny.

Finally, after lettin' my belt out a notch or two, I pushed back, took another sip of that real coffee, and let out a sigh like the beginning of a blue norther. Man, that was some meal.

Sarge just eyeballed me and my bulging gut, and give me a knowin' grin.

"She's a shore enough cook, ain't she, Boy?"

"It's a wonder some hombre ain't tried to steal her," I opined.

"Oh, they've tried, but for some reason that old woman seems to care for me. Now," he continued, "tell me about your paw."

I laid it out for him as best I knowed and, without mentioning no names, told him what I seen, and what I figured from the sign nearby.

"Damn shame," he said, "I knowed your paw and he was as good a man as they come. Reckon who'd want to bushwhack a man like that?"

I had no answers, only ideas, and a man best hold his tongue on such things less he was lookin' for trouble. No use stirrin' the pot 'til you knowed what it held.

Me and Sarge talked long into the night. We talked some about my pelts and the cost of goods, but saved the tradin' for tomorrow. He ast about my cut down holster and I showed him how it worked, but slow and easy.

I told him about ol' Rip and our winterin', and he seemed right interested in it all. Maybe he was just being kind but I figured, like everybody else, he was starved for news and company.

"Boy," he says, "You got more betwixt them ears than many a man, and you're sizin' up right good. I reckon one day you'll make your mark on this land."

Well I swelled up on hearing that from this old man who'd been around a bit. He'd fought in the war of 1812 and personally knowed General Nathan Towson, for whom Fort Towson was named. He'd fought some Indians when he first came west, and his words made me proud. I knew not to get the big head though, for that would be foolish.

"Son, these old bones are gettin' weary," Sarge finally admitted. "You can bunk in the lean-to or down to the stable in the hay, if you've a mind to."

"Thank you, Sir, but I'll just unroll out in them woods somewhere. I'm mighty comfortable there just listenin' to the night and sleepin' with the stars."

"Well, goodnight then, and don't forget to come down about a half hour past sun-up for flapjacks, sausage, and real maple syrup." Like he thought I might! My eyes liked to have popped plumb out when I heard about breakfast. With a knowin' grin, he headed off to bed.

I went out to whistle up ol' Rip and mosey up to the grove. That's when I discovered he had no thought of whuppin' that mongrel dog. Turns out that was a female and Rip just naturally made him a new friend.

"Well, Horse," I says to the roan, "Guess it's just you and me tonight."

Now I had nothin' against sleeping indoors if need be, but when the weather was right, I surely enjoyed layin' my roll out under the stars. The sounds of the breeze through the pines, the crickets stirrin' up a ruckus, or an old hooty owl askin' "who-whooo" was out there, was like music to me. A bullfrog croakin' or a night bird singin', it all fit into the puzzle that is night, and made me feel a piece of it.

I slept soundly, but any sudden changes in those sounds would wake me as sure as a baby's cry wakes his ma from a sound slumber. The darkness was like a blanket around me, warm and comfortable.

~ ~ ~ ~ ~

If Sarge thought my eyes was apoppin' when he mentioned them flapjacks, he didn't know the half of it. After putting away so much I was downright embarrassed, I reared back on that bench and dang if my shirt buttons wasn't poppin' too.

"Sarge," I asked, "ya'll wouldn't consider adopting a orphan boy now would you?"

"Sonny," he laughed, "We couldn't feed no strappin' galoot what put away that many groceries in one sittin'."

"Well, shucks, a feller can dream, cain't he?"

Sipping our coffee, we got down to talkin' trade. Sarge give me top dollar for my hides and took me down to meet Dave Billings and his wife, Sandra. Dave was the smithy, a bear of a man about six foot four, packin' around 280 pounds. We worked out a deal for shoes and some oats for the roan.

After packing up all the necessaries along with another knife, some new shirts and pants, socks, and a new round brim hat, I come out seven dollars richer than when I got there. Sarge even throwed in another meal!

"Well, now," I thought, "this tradin' business ain't hard at all."

By that afternoon, I had a pack made up for my travois and figured to hit the trail in time to camp at a likely spot a few miles north. Me and Sarge was just settin' with our coffee and jawin' when we heard horses out front and, shortly, boots on the porch. Sarge stood as the door opened, jiggling that bell.

The first man in was a squatty sorta hombre about five foot six. Unshaven for a week or so, he was totin' one of them trigger-less five shooters in a tied down holster. These guns had no trigger guard and a hidden trigger that popped out under the cylinder when the hammer was eared back. It kinda tucked into the bottom of the grip until the gun was cocked. This was another of Sam Colt's guns, but older than the Walker. Sam Walker wanted something better for the Texas Rangers, so him and Mr. Colt come up with the six shot I carried.

The second man looked so much like the first I knowed they was kin. He was maybe an inch taller and not so heavy but with the same overlarge nose, kinda broad, like somebody had swatted it with a bois d'arc post, and dark, deep sunk eyes under one long bushy brow. Weren't nothing about either of them to make a momma proud. They looked sorta familiar, but I couldn't place 'em.

"What can I do for you boys?" Sarge asked as they bellied up to the plank bar.

"Whiskey," said the taller one, "and not that rot gut Injun crap."

"I don't sell no rot gut, nor crap," says Sarge. "That'll be four bits."

"Four bits!" sputtered ugly number two. "That's robbery!"

"Mebbe so, but it ain't rotgut," says Sarge. "So pay up or drink somewheres else."

I had to hand it to that old man. There weren't no back up in him, and you could hear the steel in his voice.

Out of the corner of my eye, I seen Sarge's woman, Lawassa, standin' just inside the opening to the back cabin. She was cradling a two-barrel scattergun like she'd hold a baby child. She was outta' their sight, and listenin' close. I reckon she heard unfriendly voices and allowed she'd cover her man.

I eased closer to the wall to be less in the line of fire, if it come to that. 'Course, a scattergun ain't real friendly if you be anywhere near the business end of it.

Them yahoos musta' decided Sarge weren't interested in playin' with them, 'cause they both turned to glare at me.

"Who're you?" growled Squatty.

Now that can be considered a right unfriendly question in many places. Generally, a man told his name if and when he wanted to. Some mighty fine folks had been misunderstood, or had a grievance, in other parts and chose to change their handle when they changed their location. This was pretty much understood and most folks give their name and waited for a response. If one weren't forthcoming, or the answer was just "Slim", they just went on with their talk, no questions asked. Nosin' into other folks' business wasn't polite.

Being an overall cheerful sort, and with nothin' to hide, I simply told the man, "Stout, Jonathon Stout."

Four shaggy eyebrows seemed to raise at the same time.

"Stout?" Squatty seemed stunned. "You kin to Grayson Stout?"

"He was my Paw."

"You cain't be his brat," blurted number two, "he's just a kid."

"Well, I reckon he's growed some," Sarge interrupted.

The two uglies shared a look, then glowered at me. Squatty started in, "I reckon yore a skunk, just like Grayson was."

Now I weren't packin' iron since I seen no need in this peaceful little settlement. My colt and belt lay atop my pack in the corner so I could belt up for the trail. That didn't mean I had to back up for such talk. There's many a worse things to call a body, and a lot of men had died for less, but if a man was to hold his head up and walk tall amongst decent folks, he just couldn't abide such as that.

I eased up from that rough table and looked dead into Squatty's eyes. I was a good four or five inches taller, but thirty pounds lighter, and his arms looked like saplings.

"Them's hard words to use on a man you don't know," I said quietly. The look in my eyes must of said what I didn't, 'cause he took a step back and dropped a hand near his gun.

Right then was when Mrs. Sarge really become the prettiest woman in the country. She stepped through the entry with that scattergun leveled in the general direction of them fellers. That's aim enough for a double barrel!

I seen their throats bobble like a fishin' cork as they both swallowed hard and Sarge spoke up. "Ya'll be droppin' the guns on the bar and steppin' outside if you want to continue this conversation. Otherwise, ride out now."

"Not yet," I put in. "My paw has been dead near a year now, and nobody's ever spoke of him like that. Apologize before you go. Not for me, but for my paw."

"Damned if I will," muttered Squatty.

"Then shuck that gun or I'll get mine and we can step out."

"Won't be no gun play," allowed Sarge, "stray shots tend to get innocent folks."

"Well?" I asked, still looking him dead in the eye.

"Why you shorthorn, I'll whup you worsen I did yore paw." Squatty swore.

Then it hit me. These was the Wiggins boys. It'd been so long since I seen 'em, I hadn't recollected who they was. A red flare went off behind my eyes.

"You ain't never whupped nothin' that could fight back," I said. "Now shuck that iron or be branded a coward. It's too late for apologizin'." Giving the devil his due, he unbelted and headed for the door. His brother started to follow.

"Hold up there," Sarge stopped him, "Just leave your iron, too, so's there's no accidental shootin'." Giving Sarge a hard look and glancin' at that scattergun, he shed his colt.

I'd never had to fight before. Oh, a few tussles with other kids when we went somewheres, but no real fights. Paw had whiled away many an evenin' teaching me some boxing, and some throws the Indians favored, but I had no real experience. Still, I felt no real fear or worry. I was feeling the blood rushin' around my skull like angry bees circling a hive, and a kinda light headed feeling from what he'd said about Paw.

Havin' no experience, I wasn't ready for the sledge-hammer fist that landed upside my head as I stepped off the porch. I thought there'd be some kinda ritual like spittin' in the dust, or drawin' a line with your boot toe, but learned real quick that this was no game. Staggered, I fell sideways, but got my balance quick, and never left my feet. Wary now, I circled to my right and, shakin' the cobwebs outta' my head, raised my fists.

Squatty suddenly lowered his head and charged right at my middle, heavy arms looping to each side. I knowed I couldn't let him get me inside those monster arms with his head buried in my gut, or my back would be broke and the life squeezed outta' me before he let go.

I sidestepped as fast as I could to my left side and brung my right fist down as he rushed past. I swung it like you'd one hand a sledge, or a hatchet, and the back side of my closed fist connected with the back of his neck. It was a lucky shot 'cause I was only trying to fend him off, but I'd swung hard.

His rush, and my fist, planted him face first in the dirt of the road. Stunned, he laid there a minute, and then, shakin' his head like a sore bear, he pushed slowly up and rolled to a settin' position. Glaring at me, he rose to his feet and, more carefully, began to stalk.

Havin' slowed him down some, I now got to use some of Paw's teachin'. I had the reach on him, even if he was more powerful, so I reached out with a left and thumped him solid on his nose. His head bobbed back and he blinked a few times. I hadn't hurt him much but was testin' the water. It seemed just right, so I thumped him again, much harder.

Finally, he put his arms up and began to move some. As little as I knew of boxing, he knew less, and I hit him again with a straight left. He wasn't liking this one bit. With a growl, he swung wildly at my head. If that blow had landed, I wouldn't be tellin' you this, 'cause I'd likely be long buried. But, one of the things Paw taught me was that not getting hit was just as important as hittin' the other feller.

My feet planted, one forward, one back, it was easy to sideslip his wild swing. He'd swung so hard he kept turnin' half around when he missed, and I planted a solid left to his kidney. That brought a grunt from him as he kept goin' around, stumbling, before turnin' to face me again.

I could see in his face that he was shook up and didn't know how to come at me anymore. I could also see he was determined not to get beat by no kid. His arms up around his head, he stepped in again—and I popped him again. This time, though, I followed up with a solid right into his unprotected gut.

"Whoof." I both felt and smelt his stinkin' breath as he dropped his arms and I rattled him with a coupla quick lefts. His eyes was wide open when I set up solid and like to have busted my right hand with a hard uppercut to the end of his chin. I put everything I had into that shot.

He just stood there a second, knees locked, before I seen his eyes roll up and watched him topple like a tree. His knees never bent, he just kinda 'whoomped' face down into the dust, stirrin' up a small cloud. His brother stared, like he'd never seen such, and dropped his hand down to find only empty air at his hip. He started towards me and Sarge's voice cut the stillness. "Hold on, you!" He spoke with authority. "That's enough! He got what he ast for, so load him up and skedaddle. Ya'll ain't welcome here no more."

"You ain't seen the last of us," the standin' one glared at me as Sarge give him their guns. I just looked him in the eye, saying nothing, before turnin' my back and goin' inside.

All of a sudden I felt weak. Knees trembling, I groped for a rocker and sank into it. I felt cold sweat on my face and my arms were heavy as anvils. I weren't scared, and the anger was gone, so what was this awful weakness? Then, I realized it was just the let down after those tense, dangerous minutes I'd faced.

"Whew," Sarge breathed, mopping his brow. "Where'd you learn to fight like that?"

Handing the scattergun back to the missus, who he'd taken it from, he continued, "Boy, I've seen a few fist fights, but he never laid a hand on you 'cept once, when he caught you off guard."

"Truth be told, Sarge, I never fought for real before now. My paw taught me some stuff, but that's all."

"Well, he shore taught you enough! I never seen the like."

Lawassa brought us two mugs of coffee and this time I accepted Sarge's offer to put a slug in both. I made him take the money for mine and his while I unwound like an over-tight pocket watch.

Chapter 3

RIP WAS NOWHERE AROUND when me and the roan got ready. Both of us was well rested, well fed, and had new shoes, so we was ready to travel. I let him buck some of the sassiness out before fixin' my travois to him. It was a good load, so I knew I'd walk more on the return trip, but that was no problem. I enjoyed walkin'.

Saying 'so long' to Sarge and Lawassa, and whistling again for Rip, we turned toward the trail. Rip didn't show, so I figured he'd find me in his own time, or settle down with his new lady friend. He was a free dog, so it'd be his choice, but I would surely miss him if he stayed.

Climbing through the saddle, past the pine grove where I'd slept, I turned to look back on Pine Ridge once more. Sarge was still standin' on the porch, just watchin', and he raised a hand, once, and dropped it to his side. I taken off my new hat, circled it over my head, and replanted it. I'd sure miss those kind folks, and I reckoned they'd taken a shine to me, too. That cabin was still waitin', but nothin' else.

Being part of the trade route, this part of the trail was well traveled. Still, I saw nobody that day as I made my way north. It'd be sometime late tomorrow, or the next mornin', before I turned more east and made my way along the Kiamichi River towards my cabin on the creek. The Kiamichi ran west and south from the mountains down to the Red River, the other side of which was Texas. I'd pick it up and back track it most of the way home.

Comin' down, I had cut across country, away from the river, and wanted to see a different part of the land on my way back.

That evenin', I stripped and rubbed the roan down good, then fixed some grub. There was plenty of grass, but I knowed that horse would be missin' those oats so I surprised him with a handful out of the sack I'd got from Dave. I swear he snorted a 'thank you' after lickin' my palm clean.

The campfire weren't the same without Rip to flapjaw with, but I settled into the rhythm of the night and just listened. It's hard to be lonesome when you can hear the sounds, and the skittering, of all the night critters. The woods are never really still 'cept when a man, or other danger, is passin' through. Once I settled down with a last cup of coffee, the critters went about their business. Somewhere in the distance I could hear the insistent call of a Bob White. They must always be lookin' for something 'cause their call, rising at the end, always sounds like a question to me. Closer in, there were sounds of late movin' squirrels getting nested in after I'd disturbed them. If a man listened, and learned, he could hear many such animals movin' in the dark and know what they were doing.

Come mornin', I fried up some hog belly and warmed a couple of Lawassa's biscuits. She'd packed me enough to last me home, and put in some of her jerky and fry bread for eatin' on the trail. Sarge was a lucky man to have found that woman. Rip still hadn't showed, and I had about decided he was makin' a new home. Dang, I'd miss that mangy dog.

Anyway, me and Horse got to movin' and settled into the trail. Towards dark, I come up to the Kiamichi and turned east along the south bank. Further up, I'd cross over. The cabin was situated near a creek flowin' from the north into the river, but still a ways off.

I found a likely spot for a camp about a hundred yards back from the river amongst a grove of oaks. You didn't want to camp right on the river, 'cause the critters needed to drink, and skeeters could be bad at the right time of year. A thinkin' man would move back far enough to allow animals clear access to their usual drinkin' spots.

That night, I lay awake in my bedroll and studied on the future. The cabin and land around it would provide all I needed to live, but it would be a rough, lonesome life. A man needed more if he wanted to make his mark and leave better for those that followed him.

I was still young, but growed enough to make a livin'
just about anywhere. The problem was, I didn't know where
I wanted to go, or what I'd do when I got there. The cabin
meant security of a sort, which was somethin' I needed, but I
was getting itchy to see more and learn more of this land.
The stories and fire talk of places far distant and wild had
stirred my blood.

There was a cravin' in me I couldn't describe, but it kept
tugging at me and makin' me uncomfortable.

Visitin' with Sarge and his missus had made me realize
how much was missing in my life. The simple company of
good, decent folks was almighty powerful. Now, I had to
really bear down and start figuring out my next move. For
now, I reckoned, another year at the cabin would give me
more time to study on it. I'd heard much of the Texas Rangers and was considerin' what such a life might mean when I
drifted off to sleep.

~ ~ ~ ~ ~

I woke quickly, with all senses alert. It was late into the night
and I had sensed a change in the night sounds. Quiet. That's
what had woke me, not a new noise, but the sudden lack of
it. Shiftin' slow like, I reached out a hand and snagged my
nearby colt and powder bag. Another thing a smart man
don't do is sleep in these woods with his guns out of reach.

The fire had died down to coals and it was mighty dark
in amongst the trees. Not a critter was stirrin' nearby and I
knowed something was out there that wasn't a usual part of
the night. Not movin' at all, I just laid there and listened
hard, thinkin' it might be a big cat or somethin'.

The stamp of a horses' hoof was the first clear sound to
reach me, then I began to pick out what sounded like low
voices. "Why would anybody be sneakin' around here at
night," I wondered. Maybe they was huntin', but not many
folks hunted at night without a coon dog. I decided to just
ease further from the coals and wait 'em out.

The voices barely reached my ears, but I could tell it was two of them, and they weren't real quiet in the woods. It sounded like they was arguin' about something, and movin' closer.

"He's gotta' be around here." I barely made out the words.

"Shuttup!" hissed the other, and I thought I recognized the voice. It was the Wiggins! Now what was they doin' looking for somebody in these parts late at night? I reckoned it was me they was huntin', and I didn't want to disappoint them none. "You boys lookin' for somebody?" I spoke quietly from the dark.

Silence greeted my words. Nothin' more was said, but I could tell from the sounds of their passing that they had split up. One was circlin' to get on my flank. The other, trying to be quiet, but not havin' much luck with the underbrush, eased the other way and kept comin' in.

I moved to another dark shadow and, colt in hand, waited. Just as I glimpsed a rustle of brush to my left, flame stabbed the darkness from the other side and I heard a bullet strike near where I'd been. "Maybe these fools will shoot each other," I hoped.

I didn't fire back since I didn't have either of 'em located for sure. It seemed like a long time passed before I heard more sounds, but it must have been only a minute or two. They still hadn't spotted me either, but a man with a gun, in the dark of night, was a dangerous thing. No matter the odds.

Again, flame shredded the dark as three sharp reports cut the stillness. Each was aimed at a different area of the camp in an effort to get me with a lucky shot. I was hunkered down near the base of a huge old oak and felt safe enough for now, but knew they'd get me sooner or later if they both commenced firin' like that. Seeing where the muzzle blast had sprouted, I fired two shots in that direction, and again shifted positions before reloading the two empties out of my belt pouch.

It sounded like a small war had erupted in those woods. The shots came from both sides and reminded me of a string of firecrackers I seen once over at Fort Smith. The 'thunk' of bullets hittin' the trees all around where I'd fired from was a scary sound as I lay flat out on the ground. I wondered what sound they'd make hittin' my body.

This situation was gettin' right hairy and I weren't sure how to go about getting out of it. If I moved, they'd likely hear or see me and it'd all be over. But, if I stayed, they'd sooner or later get me. It seemed my options was downright limited, and none of 'em looked real good. It got quiet as a graveyard again and I figured they was both reloadin' so I taken that chance to fire off two shots at each of them.

"Damn!" I heard Squatty's voice off to the right and a scramble as he sought better cover.

"Lord," I thought, "If you got anybody lookin' out for me, now'd be a good time for them to step in."

Snakin' around to the other side of that oak, I snagged a stick with my buckskins. It let go with a slight 'snap', and the fusillade started up again. This time, I weren't so lucky. I felt the bite of the bullet when it hit my leg above the knee like a hammer blow. The last thing I felt was a blow to my head, and it snapped sideways to connect with the trunk of the tree. Then everything went black.

I don't know how long I was out, but I slowly come around, hearin' their voices. Not a hair did I twitch as I tried to overcome the pounding pain in my head. Once it subsided a little, I felt my leg throbbin', too. They were goin' through my pack and swearin' at the little bit of money I carried. Most of my money I'd sewed into the waist of my britches. What they'd found was the last of the seven dollars I'd got from Sarge.

I knowed I was hurt bad. It felt like my leg was still bleedin', and my hair was matted from blood on my head. I could feel the stickiness on my face as I lay still and listened.

"He musta' had more than this," Squatty ranted.

"Oh, hell, just take what we can use or sell and let's get outta' here," replied Number Two. I was later to learn their names were Bart and Bert, but never knowed which was which.

"What about him?"

"Guess we'll have to make sure he's dead." The words brought a chill to me. Murderin' a helpless man was about as low as a body could get, and these two was talkin' about it like they was discussin' supper. I fought the darkness that again tried to take away my conscious thought, and forced my throbbing head to function. There had to be something I could do, if I could only think! If I moved, it'd only draw their attention and get me killed, but I couldn't just lay there like a helpless baby and let them murder me.

Easing one eye open a crack, I seen that they were on the other side of the clearing, pawin' through my pack. Maybe if I could move real slow I could ease into the woods before they noticed. Tensing my muscles to try pushing backwards a little, I could barely stifle a groan. My leg burnt like fire, and even that little bit of effort brought sweat poppin' out on my throbbing head. Getting to cover was gonna be a torturous thing.

Right then was when Squatty said, "Forget it. None of this is much good to us. Let's take care of him and get outta' here." I opened my eyes to watch him turn toward me and draw his gun. If he was gonna shoot a helpless man, he'd have to do it with my eyes on him so he could see the contempt in them.

"So, our big man is awake." He drew a bead on my head. Tryin' to raise my head, I couldn't stop the groan this time. Well, I'd done my best, and would die like a man.

All hell broke loose in them woods! The thrashin' and growlin' was horrible to hear. I thought a bear had somehow snuck up on us 'til I seen a flash of yeller hide tear into Squatty. Rip! That big dog had come after all.

Rip was chewin' on Squatty's arm and shakin' that big man around like a rag mop. Squatty was squallin' like a pig for his brother to get that thing off him, and number two was wavin' his gun around, tryin' to get something to shoot at without hittin' Squatty. Sudden as a rattler strike, Rip let go of the mangled arm, and leaped on the other man. He seemed to know to go for the gun hand, and he got him a grip.

Though it was too dark to see clear, I could tell Squatty was holdin' that tore up arm and swearin' like crazy. About now, the other feller went to bellerin' for help.

Round and round ol' Rip took him, tearin' at that arm the while. Then, he let go and looked around at Squatty again. That was the last straw! Both of 'em broke for their horses. Forget any thought of robbin' or killin', they was only interested in gittin'!

Rip let 'em go and came to look me over. I couldn't help but grin at that onery, mangy old hound. He was hell on wheels when he got stirred up. He lopped out his tongue and licked the matted blood on my face.

"Thanks, Rip," I said, and faded back into darkness.

~ ~ ~ ~ ~

My stomach woke me. It was rumblin' something awful as the wonderful smell of fresh cookin' wafted under my nose. My eyes opened slowly and I looked straight up into the branches of an ancient elm.

"Well, am I dead," I asked myself. "Is this what heaven is like?" The sounds of people and animals began to penetrate my numbed mind.

"If this is heaven, it's awful busy." I responded to my own question.

Talkin' to yourself and then answerin' is the first sign of goin' crazy, I'd been told. It figured, 'cause none of this made sense right now. I decided to just lay there and let my surroundings come to me. Voices, some in an unknown tongue, dogs barkin', kids playin', and the strident sound of some poor soul gettin' tongue-lashed by an angry woman.

"Okay, This I can understand. But, where am I and how did I get here?"

Letting myself relax, it began to come back. The Wiggins brothers, the gunfight, Rip. Rip! Where was Rip? That mutt had saved my life. I prayed he was all right.

Still layin' quiet, I considered my circumstance. I was alive, number one. I felt a binding on my leg, which told me it must be bandaged, number two. Third, my head hurt somethin' awful, and was also bandaged, but that again told me I was livin'. I quit countin' and tried to figure the rest. The big one had been answered, I was alive! Where I was I had no idea, but my ears told me there was people around. Who brought me here was also a question, but somebody had bandaged and cared for me.

I recollected Rip tearin' into them yahoos as they was gettin' ready to commit cold blooded murder on my person, but nothing after that. Somebody, somehow, had taken the trouble to care for me, and I'd sure like to be able to thank 'em for it. The leaves on that great elm began to quiver as the freshening breeze touched them. My stomach growled again, and I went back to sleep.

My next wakenin', I was almost sure I was in heaven 'cause an angel was bent over me with a look of worry in her dark, lovely eyes. One hand I felt under my head while the other was tryin' to spoon warm liquid into my mouth. I reckoned this couldn't be heaven, though, 'cause I could also feel the soft warmth of her breast against my cheek. When she looked into my wide-open eyes, she jumped and dropped both the spoon and my head. That hurt!

Not the spoon, 'cause it only hit my chest and weren't real hot, but my head wasn't so lucky, it bounced off the hard ground. As I was blinkin' the water—not tears mind you—outta my eyes, she picked up my poor, abused head and cradled it to her bosom.

"So sorry," the angel spoke, "You're awake."

I weren't sure if she was sorry for droppin' me or sorry I was awake but, rightfully, I didn't care. This was the prettiest creature I'd ever laid eyes on and she could bounce my punkin' anytime she wanted to, as long as I could look into those eyes.

Both hands now cradled my throbbing head and she kinda rocked, like she was rockin' a baby, as she held me. With apologies to mommas everywhere, I was as entranced with the tenderness of her bosom as with the rockin'.

My breath was hung up somewhere deep inside while I studied those liquid eyes. Her cheeks were high and tan. The long ebony hair flowed loosely over her shoulders and brushed my forehead as she continued to rock. Her full lips, pursed in concern, began to move as a crooning sound came from her in a language I didn't know. It reminded me of a lullaby I heard a woman sing to her baby once, a long time ago. I remembered it 'cause I was wishin' my Ma could have sung it to me.

The rockin', crooning, and soothing touch must have had the desired effect 'cause, with an angel holdin' me, I drifted out again.

Chapter 4

MY GOD! Somethin' awful was attackin' me!

'Sluuurp'! Again it got me! Rough, sloppy, and smelly, it slopped over my face. Ugh!

Openin' my eyes I saw, not my angel, but a wet, black, runny nose surrounded by yeller fuzz. Then that long, pink tongue reached out again.

"Rip," I hollered, "No!" At least I tried to holler, but found very little voice. I reckon if you don't use it, you lose it. At least, that's what Paw always said about muscles. Personally, I reckoned it was just his way of gettin' me to work harder. Rip cocked his big old head to one side the way dogs do, and eyeballed me, curious like. That huge tongue snaked out again but, this time, he didn't lick me with it.

"Thank you, Lord," I breathed. I swear he grinned at me!

"You no good, mangy, flea-bit, worthless, slobberin', wonderful dog, you." I almost cried. "I love you, but don't kiss me no more, ever!" That ugly mutt just cocked his head to the other side and appeared to be considerin' what kinda fool he'd hooked up with.

My surroundings had changed again. Now I was inside some kind of cabin, or hut. I could see saplings holdin' up a sod roof overhead. Turnin' my head a little left, I could make out a small fire surrounded with rocks, and a pot hung on a shepherd's crook over it. Whatever was in that pot smelled good enough to set my gut to growlin' again.

While I was contemplatin' whether I could get to that pot, a shaft of light broke across my eyes and somebody came in. When my dazzled eyes had settled down somewhat, I seen an old Indian man leanin' over the pot and tasting the contents with a wooden spoon.

"Hungry," I mumbled.

Turning a weathered face, dominated by wise old eyes, in my direction, he cracked a gap-toothed smile. "You awake."

The last time I'd heard those words, I was seein' a totally different face.

"Food," I tried again.

"Good. You eat."

"Well," I thought, "That's a start."

He fetched a wood bowl and ladled me up some of that food. It was only lukewarm, and a bit greasy, but was some of the best stew I'd ever had, regardless. I chucked it down like I hadn't et in a week, which might be so for all I knowed. When I'd scrounged the last bite and tilted the bowl to my lips to get that final drop of rich gravy, I pushed it back at him and said, "More."

"No more now. More not good." He reached out a gnarled old hand and patted my stomach. I knew he meant my stomach probably couldn't handle more, but I still felt like I was starved. I gave in to his wisdom and tried to be satisfied, but it weren't easy.

"Where am I?"

"My people. You hurt bad. Be okay now. You safe."

Pointing to himself, he said, "Owl feather, you?"

"Jonathon," I answered.

"Jonathon. Good. Okay. Jonathon." Each word a separate statement, then that gap toothed grin, again.

The throbbing in my leg reminded me I'd been shot. At least ol' Rip had come out of it without a scratch, that onery devil.

One hand went to my head and felt the bandage there. Probing with my fingers, I felt a large knot on the left side and another, very sore, on the right. This one had a dent in it so I reckoned they had shot me there and that had knocked my head into the tree. Only a half-inch between livin' and dyin'. One of the mysteries of life, I reckon.

The old man had moved back to the pot and was eatin' out of the same bowl he'd served me in. I wanted to ask him about the angel, but figured it best to hold my tongue for now. I studied him in the dim light. In a way, he reminded me of Sarge. The way he held himself, his manner, and the look of ageless wisdom in those dark eyes, spoke of a long and honorable life.

He was once a large man, now withered with age and countless sorrows. His hair, still dark, hung loosely down his back and glistened with the fat he'd brushed into it. A soft, loose fitting, buckskin shirt, adorned with a few colored beads, covered his once large chest. It had the buckskin fringes common on the front, back, and arms. Some thought they was just for decoration, but those fringes helped to drain away the rain and keep the wearer dry. Below that, he wore dark britches sorta like cavalry trousers without the stripe down the leg.

I watched him eat from that stewpot and wondered at the history that had shaped this one man, and what legacy he'd be leavin' when he was gone. This set me to thinkin' again, and askin' the same questions of myself. Right now, though, I didn't dwell on them. Turning my attention back to Owl Feather, I watched as he, like I had, tipped the bowl to his lips to savor the last drop.

"Never waste, never want." My paw's words came, un-bidden, back to me. All those sayin's of Paw's, which I had thought little of before, began to make sense now. Rather than scold or lecture, Paw had a way of tryin' to help me see wisdom in simple things. It was amazing how much smarter Paw got as I got older. He'd taught me a lot in a few years.

" A penny saved is better than a penny earned, you don't have to work for it." Now, that made a lot of sense.

"A man is as good as his word." This I now understood to be good or bad, depending on how good was a man, or his word. You couldn't trust a man with a mean spirit, and a man who wouldn't keep his word was generally no good. Folks in these parts sorted 'em out pretty quick. There was lots of such things that hadn't stuck at the time, or so I'd thought, but had much meaning to a man tryin' to make his way on a good, straight path.

Owl Feather sucked the last drop from that bowl, peered into the pot, as if to gauge his options, and set the bowl aside. He turned to look at this strange white man who had somehow come into his home, then eased over to my side. His fingers poked at my leg. It was real sore, and I jerked away.

That gap tooth grin spoke before he did, "Okay."

"No, it hurts bad."

"Hurt okay, get better."

Regardless of my recent philosophy of thought, I weren't ready to accept that hurt was good. Especially since it was me doin' the hurtin'. Still, I reasoned, this old man had fed me before he ate, which told me somethin' of his character.

He reached out and snagged a water bag, and brung it to my lips. I drank deeply. What with eatin', drinkin', pokin', and thinkin', I was wore out. I went back to sleep.

~ ~ ~ ~ ~

My angel was back. The soft sweet sound of her humming was the first thing to register on my consciousness as I slowly came awake. Cracking one eye and easing my head real slow like to the side, so as not to disturb her, I seen she was facin' away from me. Opening my eyes fully, I watched while she went about sweepin' out the cabin with a stalk broom. The floor was packed earth, but as clean as it could be made.

Her hair shone blue-black like the wings of a raven, and her movements looked like dancin' to me. Since the blanket at the door was pulled aside, I could see highlights like fireflies in that waist length hair when it swept side to side in time with her movement.

Layin' abed, I couldn't rightly judge her size, but figured she was short, about five foot two or so, and slender. Slender and supple, like a willow, but with a womanly curve beginning at her waist and flowing into well-shaped hips. Her fawn colored dress ended just below the knee, and showed strong, shapely calves. I knowed I shouldn't be lookin' upon this girl like I was, but couldn't help myself.

She turned a little and cast a look in my direction. I froze, feeling my blood begin to boil like an unwatched pot, but she kept on with her sweepin' and humming. I reckon it was dim enough in my corner and, what with the full light hittin' mostly where she stood, she didn't see I was awake. The pain in my leg and head had eased, but they was nothin' anyway, compared to the pain in my chest just now. It felt like a grown bear was sittin' on it, and my breath was hard to draw in.

She was beautiful! That heart shaped face with the pert nose, high cheekbones, and almond eyes set my poor heart to flutterin' like a drunk butterfly. Her slenderness only accented small pert bosoms, cupped by a slightly too tight dress.

When she turned to face me fully, I knowed I was in love! No matter her name, 'My Angel' she'd always be, in my heart. Finally seeing my eyes open, she stopped her sweepin' and stood stock still, those enchanting eyes searchin' my face. I seen a strange look come over her, and thought something was wrong, but she just stood and stared. I stared back.

The grumblin' of my dang stomach finally broke the spell and, with suddenly downcast eyes, she hurried to the fire and scooped out a heapin' bowl of stew. I had been so caught up in her beauty I hadn't noticed the smell this time. My belly did though, and commenced such an uproar you'd of thought there was a wild boar fight goin' on in there.

Smiling at the noise I was makin', she knelt beside me and offered me the bowl. I coulda' waited all day, just to look at her, but figured I'd better quiet the rumblin's before they got worse. As I reached for the bowl our fingers touched and fire shot up my arm. It left me with that tingly feeling you get right after lightin' strikes nearby during a storm, and kinda weak inside. She must of felt somethin' too, 'cause her eyes opened wider and she jerked a little.

For a long minute she knelt there, each of us holding onto that bowl, afraid to move, and just lookin' in each others' eyes. Tired of waitin', my innards complained again and, without a word, she turned away and rose to her feet.

"*Impa*," she said, motioning to the bowl. "Eat."

Keepin' her back to me, she went about her chores while I commenced to eat. I was kinda glad she wasn't looking, 'cause I couldn't take my eyes off her and didn't want to appear rude. Whenever she did sneak a look my way, I quickly looked down at the bowl until I sensed she'd quit lookin'.

"Jonny boy," I says to myself, "That there is some kinda woman."

"Yep," came an unwanted thought, "and you got as much chance with her as a daisy in a hailstorm."

Seeming to forget I was there, except for a peek now and then, she commenced humming again while she went about her work. To my ears her voice was sweeter than the lonesome call of a whippoorwill in the dusk of a spring day. Shortly, she came and refilled my bowl, being careful not to let our fingers touch this time.

"What's your name?" I asked.

"Mourning Dove, in English."

"A lovely name," I said.

"*Yakoke*, thank you." Her words had a musical lilt and you could tell English wasn't her first language, but she spoke it well.

"This is your home?"

"No, home of *Amafo*, my grandfather." She replied.

"*Amafo* is your grandfather's name?"

"*Kiyo,* no." She giggled, "*Amafo* means 'my grandfather' in my tongue, Choctaw."

That little giggle set my poor heart to flutterin' again.

"*Kiyo*," she continued, "means 'no'. I will be your *ikanachi*, or teacher. You learn my language."

"*Amafo*," I tried it. "Grandfather."

"Good, *achukma*," she said.

Her name was a real mouthful in Choctaw. It seems there really weren't a single word for it. Some words just weren't in their language. She later told me that for 'turkey', you said 'tall chicken'. There was a word for chicken, but not turkey. Seemed strange to me but heck, I had a lot to learn yet.

"What about your mother and father?"

A shadow crossed her lovely features. "They cross the great river to a happy place. They are with loved ones. Cannot speak their names or spirits get restless and try to come back. *Amafo* is all family now."

"I'm sorry."

"No sorrow, they are in a good place. Someday I go there, see them again."

After I finished my second helpin' of stew, she came to sit with me and talk awhile. She told me of her people, and her grandfather, Owl Feather.

It seems her people, the warriors at least, may have more than one name in their life. A youngster may be called "Slow Running Turtle", but become "Brave Bear" after proving himself in battle, or on the hunt. As they age, it may change again, as was the case with Owl Feather.

Braves who wear the owl feather in their hair are said to be strong of spirit, and can combat witches. An eagle feather means strength and wisdom, and is usually worn by a chief, or leader. Turkey feathers indicate a great hunter, while the wearer of a buzzard feather was said to be a healer. I'd thought, like most people, that these feathers was just decoration, not knowin' they showed social position in the tribe.

When I asked, Mourning Dove explained that she had gone to the missionary school to learn English, and learn about Jesus. She was a believer, but felt her Christian beliefs were compatible with her ancestral beliefs, too.

Owl Feather, she told me, understood most English but, being an onery old man, would speak it only when he had to. I could hear in her tone how much love she had for him, even as she called him 'onery'. It was kinda like me callin' Rip a mangy mutt, or somethin'.

Before she had to go tend to other duties, she checked my wounds again, and put on new dressings. That poultice didn't smell particular good, but I reckon it was workin' just fine.

"Tomorrow you walk some," she said in leaving.

~ ~ ~ ~ ~

I weren't sure my eyes was open 'til I noticed the grayness seeping through the cracks in the cabin walls. The tang of fresh dew told me it was early mornin'. Layin' quiet, I felt around me and found I was on a low bunk covered with several layers of robes and furs. Somebody had gone to a lot of trouble to make me comfortable.

Without strainin' too much, I tested my leg. Sore as all get out, and swole up pretty big, but I weren't in no danger of dyin' I reckoned. Feelin' my head, I determined it'd be awhile afore I wore my new hat, but it weren't as bad as before.

I was hungry again but the fire was cold and there was no smell of cookin'. Easing off my bunk, I tried standin'. Well, there weren't no foot races in my immediate future, but I could hobble some on it. I did feel mighty weak, though.

Easing my way out the door, I surveyed the camp. There was several cabins around, and scattered pits for communal cookin'. Wisps of smoke testified to some live coals that would take only tinder, and a blow, to fire up.

A scrawny brown cur that had been nosin' around across the way took notice of me and commenced to bark. Dogs in Indian camps usually knew better than to bark at anybody inside the camp, but I reckon he took me for a stranger and set out to warn others.

About then, ol' Rip come around the corner, nosed my hand, and stared at that other dog. He taken a step in that direction, growlin' real low, and that dog just tucked tail and hushed. I reckon Rip already had him a reputation in these parts. Rip looked up at me and give me that lop-tongue look of his, mighty pleased with hisself. Rubbin' his ears, I took in the camp.

There was a total of seven cabins, with one in the middle bein' larger and better built than the rest. This, I was to learn, was the council lodge. In the Choctaw tribe, only warriors were permitted in the council lodge, and women were never to enter. I learned, also, that the women had plenty to say about things, but said it at home. They just never meddled publicly in the business of the tribe.

Mourning Dove and Owl Feather taught me lots, later, about the runnin' of the tribe, and their customs. One thing I shore approved of was the notion that the women did all of the work around camp, while the young'uns gathered wood and learned their roles in the camp. The boys was good little hunters with blowguns made from reeds. They'd take a reed and slit it down the side to get slivers, then sharpen these slivers and put a little tuft of something soft on them to make darts. They was real good at hittin' birds and rabbits and such. Later, they was taught to bow hunt, and then to use guns, if they had 'em.

The men? Well, their job was to fish and hunt. Now that was a job I could get into. Really though, it weren't as easy as it sounds. You often had to go far afield, and walk miles and miles for days on end to get enough game. Then you had to dress it, skin it, and tote it all back. A man didn't want to hunt out all the game near camp so you'd head out in different directions and travel a piece before huntin'. Like I said, many of their customs I found strange, but this one—I reckon I liked it.

By askin' what I thought was sly questions, I also learned about their way of courtin'. It seemed you could either chunk rocks at a girl you liked, or leave little gifts on her bed. Now I don't claim to know a lot about women, but I reckon anybody could figure this one out. Maybe if you was real young, and just puppy lovin', chunkin' rocks would do the trick, but I never figured on chunkin' no rock at Mourning Dove, no sir!

One part bothered me. If she accepted the gifts, then his family was supposed to give gifts to her family. I didn't have no family, and was some worried for awhile until I learned they had a way around that one. I could give gifts to her uncles. Well, she didn't have no uncles, so now what? I figured it'd never get done 'til one of the women told me the men had been joshin' me, and the gift could go to any man in her family if'n she didn't have no uncles. Whew!

Anyways, I finally got the straight of it. If her family took the gifts, then me and her could walk together. If we decided to tie the knot, she'd pick a day and I had to show up at her house, give her a head start, then try to catch her on foot. If she was caught, we was married; if not, I had to give it up and they'd give back what I brung 'em. I figured if my leg was well, I could catch her easy. 'Course, this was all a ways off; I just wanted to tell you how it all was supposed to go.

I learned, in time, that these was a fine, honest, and fun lovin' people. You could leave your prize knife layin' outside and, if it moved at all, it'd be brought back to you. There was no tolerance for stealin', lyin', or laziness. Now you could steal from an enemy and be proud of it, but never from your own people. It's too bad more white folks didn't think that way.

As for the fun, these folks played more pranks on each other than I ever heard of. And the joshin' goin' on, you never seen the like. They was always givin' one another some cause to laugh. I surely did enjoy their company whilst I was healin', and even more after I was accepted and made the butt of some of those jokes. I got my licks in, too; don't think I didn't.

Overall, this was a right pleasant place to be. Some things was different, but you couldn't find a better people to spend time with.

Well, folks was beginnin' to stir, and my leg was startin' to feel like somebody had stuck a hot poker in it, so I slipped on back inside, thinkin' not to bother Owl Feather. 'Course, he was already up and stirrin' up the fire, so I just eased on over to my bed and sat down.

"Mourning Dove come soon," he said. "She cook."

"That's fine, thanks."

"How leg?"

"Better," I says, "It still hurts pretty bad, though."

"Bad wound. Almost die. Lose much blood." He always spoke in short statements.

"Who found me?"

"I find. Hear many guns in night. Next morning I look, I find."

"Thank you."

"Okay," he replied.

Gradually I got the story from him of how he'd found me and Rip wouldn't let him near. Being wise in the ways of animals as well as people, he just squatted down right there and talked soft to ol' Rip for a long time. Finally, he said, Rip figured he would do me no harm and knew I needed help of some kind, so he let him come to me, keepin' a watchful eye on him all the while.

I'd lost much blood and my head wound was bad. He didn't know if I'd live, but gathered some medicine root called Tumeric, or Goldenseal, boiled it up to make a poultice, and bathed my wounds before wrapping them. Then he spooned some of the tea down me.

He gathered my belongings and stayed right there with me for four days before deciding I could travel, all the while bathing me, spoonin' what broth he could into me, and doctorin' my wounds. I was out the whole time. Somehow, he managed to roll me onto that travois and get me here. My first recollection was when he'd left me under the elm to get Mourning Dove to prepare my bed. That was near a week after I was shot. Then, he says, I was mostly out for the next week or so.

It hit me then how much I owed this old man. Without him and his caring enough to fix up a stranger like that, I'd be another of those unmarked piles of bones. It also hit me how much I owed that Wiggins clan, or at least the brothers.

Chapter 5

THE NEXT FEW WEEKS was spent mendin' and gettin' to know the folks in the camp. As I got better I taken to slippin' off into the woods and practicin' my gun work. I never belted up in camp, but slung it over my shoulder as if it didn't really count for much. One day Mourning Dove ast me about it.

"Why you carry gun into forest?"

"Well," I replied, "Just in case of critters, or maybe some game."

Lookin' in my eyes, she frowned and said, "Okay, you say so."

I knew I hadn't put nothin' over on her and felt bad about tryin', but didn't think she'd understand that I was makin' sure I was ready if I ever crossed trails with them fellers. And I was pretty sure I would. For a big country, it could be pretty small, too.

Other than gun practice, most of my time was spent talkin' with Owl Feather and Mourning Dove. I got to meet Little Fawn, the best friend of Mourning Dove. She was a little younger, but just about as pretty. Her and Mourning Dove did pert near everything together.

Owl Feather brought me to meet John Leaping Deer. He was one of the best hunters and warriors of the camp. It's hard to tell sometimes, with the Indians, how old they might be, but I figured him for mid twenties. He was not real large, but well muscled and lean as whipcord. After we jawed a few times, I figured him for a right good man. He spoke well of his family, as well as the other people of his village, and seemed particular fond of Owl Feather and Mourning Dove. It was he who brought meat to their fire, and took care of what necessaries they couldn't manage.

In return, Owl Feather taught him of the spirits and shared the wisdom of his ageless people with him. We got on right well, and I learned to respect and admire him. I was to learn a lot from him, and even come to love him as a brother.

Most folks know of the trail of tears of the Cherokee people when they was forcibly removed from their homes in the east and made to travel in terrible conditions, with little food or drink, to their assigned lands in the Indian Territories, but few talk about the Choctaw trail of tears. Takin' nothin' away from the sufferin' of the good Cherokee people, for they lost more loved ones than any other tribe, the Choctaw, and other tribes, suffered badly too. I weren't really mindful of this 'til I heard the story from Owl Feather. He wasn't puttin' blame on nobody, but just tellin' his story like I'm tellin' you mine.

The Choctaw people had lived in the lovely lands to the east for what seemed like forever, according to Owl Feather. Along with the Cherokee and Seminole, they shared much of their language, and the lands. After the coming of the whites, they begun to get more involved with self-government, but kept their council ways of conductin' business. The people chose the council, and the council chose the chiefs and leaders.

About twenty summers ago, Owl Feather told me, the tribes was told they'd have to move. Seems the government was goin' to ban their culture and make some of their doin's illegal if they stayed. The councils said the people didn't accept this, but the United States government got the chiefs to sign a treaty, against the vote of the people and the councils.

So, the move had to be made. Some stayed and tried to blend in with the white folks, but could never have a good life there.

Finally, nearly all of the Choctaw moved to the territory set aside for them in the west, or what was then the western lands. Now, we know there are far greater lands further west than was really well known then.

In what was to become typical of government planning, they decided to move the people in groups of a few thousand at a time, but near the time of winter. This only made it far worse, 'cause they not only had to deal with lack of food and such, but with the weather. That sure was a poor decision by somebody.

Anyways, there was several hundred that died from the weather, drowned tryin' to cross rivers, and sickness brought about by not havin' good food. The folks who were paid to provide for them sometimes just dumped rotten foodstuff by the side of the trail they was to follow, and left it there for them to find.

Like I said, maybe it weren't as bad as the Cherokee was treated, but bad enough at that. I'd hate to be told I had to leave my home, crops, animals and land to the use of another, and be forced to move somewheres I had no intent on goin'. I reckon I'd of had to fight, but these was a peace lovin' people and felt like they had to follow the treaty their chiefs signed, even if they hadn't wanted it.

This story made me ashamed of what my people had done to theirs. It just weren't right to make people move off land they'd been on for so long they couldn't even tell how long it had been. It was done now, but I like to think I'd of fought agin' it in the government if I'd of been there then. Maybe lots of folks was ashamed after they seen what happened to these good people. I hope so.

By the time summer was about half over, I was startin' to feel some better, and get around pretty good. I'd taken to walkin' some with Leaping Deer, and spendin' more time out and about. It was also about the time I decided to court Mourning Dove.

I was gettin' fearful some brave would sneak in ahead of me and take her for his girl, and I couldn't let that happen. Little did I know she had already set her cap for me, and had asked the wise old Owl Feather if he thought it would work out. He told her to follow her heart and everything would be just fine. I'm proud that wise old man felt that way. Shortly after my wounds had healed up some, Owl Feather asked me about my folks.

"Why you alone in mountains, Jonathon?"

"I got no family now, Owl Feather. I never knew my mother, and Paw was killed last year."

"No brothers or sisters?"

"Nope, it's just me. My folks' families live far away, back east, and I never knew 'em."

"Um, not good to be alone so young. You must be strong to live alone like that."

"I just did what I had to do. When you find yourself in that situation, you think only of survival. I reckon Paw taught me enough to make a go of it, but I sure missed havin' folks around."

"Ump." He kind of grunted, and said no more.

~ ~ ~ ~ ~

One mornin' I sneaked into the cabin of the family of Little Fawn. That's where Mourning Dove was sleepin' since I'd taken her bed. It weren't right, she said, for a maiden to share a cabin with a man not her kin. I had offered to bunk out, but she wouldn't hear of it and, besides, she said, Little Fawn's parents loved havin' her there. She earned her keep by helpin' with the chores, but taken her meals with me and Owl Feather.

Anyway, I snuck in there and put a shiny purple stone on her bed. I'd found it years ago in the hills near our stream, and had carried it ever since. It was wore smooth by bein' in my pockets so long, and by my handlin' of it. For some reason, the holdin' and rubbin' of it had always give me a peaceful feeling as I watched the light bounce off its' colors like sunlight bouncin' off a field of flowers.

I was real nervous to see if she'd keep it, or bring it back to me like it had just been lost. I spent a real itchy day just waitin' to see what she'd do. Towards sundown, after eatin', and while we was sittin' quiet like to enjoy the dusk, she eased it out of her pocket and commenced to rubbin' it between her thumb and fingers.

"Thank you, Jonathon."

My heart like to have jumped plumb outta' my throat. She was keepin' it! "You . . . you . . . you're welcome." I finally got it out.

"Very beautiful."

"Yes," I sounded like a frog croakin', "I always liked it."

Well, folks, let me assure you of somethin'. My wound might have healed up, but I still don't think I coulda' wore my hat for a while. My head swole up with joy, and I strutted around there like a young rooster who'd just learned he could crow. Man, I was proud.

That next mornin' Owl Feather found my paw's pocket-knife on his bunk. He looked sideways at me just sittin', all innocent like, on my bed. Without another look, nor a word, he opened up the blades, tested 'em with his thumb, admired all sides of it, and then slipped it in his pocket.

Whew! I hadn't known 'til then that I musta' been holdin' my breath for a full minute. I had just forgot to breathe while he was inspectin' that knife. I knew if he returned it, that'd mean he didn't think I was good enough for his granddaughter, or he didn't want me in his family. I'm glad I was sittin', or I might of fell down from weak knees.

After that, me and Mourning Dove taken to walkin' along the trails around the village and talkin' a blue streak. She taught me more and more of the language and I was gettin' right good at it, she said. I know I was findin' it easier to talk with Owl Feather since he didn't like to talk in English less'n he had to.

"You sure you want to get hitched to a feller like me?" I asked her one day.

"Jonathon, you are the man my heart wishes to be with. It was decided for me soon after you arrived."

"Well, you know you are my Angel, and I'd do anything for you, but I have nothin' to my name 'cept what you see and a run-down cabin in the hills."

"We are young," she said, "and we will not worry about such things. They will come in time. For now, you alone are enough for me."

"How do you want to marry?" I asked her. "Do we go down to the mission?"

"We can marry at the mission if you wish, or we can marry in our family tradition. This would please *Amafo*."

"Then let's please him. He is most important to me, next to you. I know our God will accept us either way. Besides, your people were marrying long before mine ever came across the oceans, so it's good enough for me."

A sweet smile and the soft touch of her lips to mine told me I had said the right thing.

Well, it weren't long before me and Mourning Dove tied the knot. I'm sure she didn't run as fast as she could, but it was still fun tryin' to catch up with her in the woods. I was sure we were destined to be a happy couple; no one could ask for a more lovin' and caring woman, and she was still my angel. She had made me up a buckskin outfit for our wedding that was bleached to pure white. With a few beads on the front, it was a mighty handsome outfit. Little did I know what it would mean to me later.

After a full day of festivities, we decided to take a honeymoon trip to my old cabin, to show her where I was brought up. We loaded up and headed out that same day, and took a slow, meanderin' way to the clearing where the cabin was. When we got there, a couple of days later, that old cabin was gone. Somebody had torched it and the lean-to, and there was nothin' left but a pile of ashes and the chimney stickin' up.

Lookin' around, I couldn't find much sign but, in a sheltered area, I did see what looked to be the prints of a horse with one kicked out hoof. The same men who killed my Paw might have done this dirty work.

I didn't lose much in the way of material goods, only some clothes and such, but I sure hated that our family bible, and Paw's books, was gone. That bible held the last link with my Ma, and Paw said she had treasured it. In it was written their birth dates, and mine, along with their wedding day. It also held the names and birthdays of their kin. It was a huge loss to me.

Standing by my side, Mourning Dove put her arm around me and pulled me close. "Oh, Jonathon, I am so sorry. You have lost everything."

"No, with you I have everything. There were books I loved to read, and the bible that belonged to my mother, but nothing else of importance."

Seein' how I was affected, she suggested we move on to the river and continue our trip. With one last look around, we walked hand in hand down to Paw's grave. Standin' over it, rememberin' how he'd come to be there, made me downright mad, and sad that he'd never know Mourning Dove, or see our happiness.

"Paw," I said, "this is my bride, Mourning Dove. I hope you and Ma can look down and see her 'cause she is my whole life now. We hope to fill our cabin with love, happiness, and children. You taught me how to make it in the world, how to be a good man, and I hope to always make you proud."

With that last goodbye, we left, never to return.

Chapter 6

WE SPENT ANOTHER WEEK just seein' the land, spending much time talkin' of our lives, and what the future might hold for us. Mourning Dove wondered aloud if I might get bored with the slow pace of living amongst her people, but I assured her that I was very happy there, and learning to love and respect them all.

Before we headed home, I took her to Pine Ridge to meet Sarge, Lawassa, Dave, and Sandra. Boy howdy, did she get a welcome. Lawassa just hugged her up real tight and Sarge, with a huge grin, insisted on huggin' her too before he poured us a shot of his finest brandy. This was some he kept stashed just for the finest of friends or occasions, and it was good.

"A toast to our newlywed friends," he crowed, "and to a long, happy life and a full cabin." He sneaked a grin at me and I knew I was blushin' to beat all. Doggone him, anyway.

Dave and Sandy came over that evenin' and we all sat around in Sarge and Lawassa's cabin behind the store, tellin' tall tales and catchin' up on goin's on. Sarge was madder'n a she bear with cubs when he heard of what them Wiggins boys had done to me, but he called up ol' Rip and give him a big chunk of venison for savin' my life.

Me, him, and Dave snuck in a couple of more snorts of that brandy, but none of us had too much. When Sarge started to sneak another, Lawassa just lifted her brows and he put that bottle right back down. Not a word was said, but he got the message loud and clear. It made me kinda grin at him and he told me to shut up, even though I hadn't spoken. We all laughed at that.

Well, me and Mourning Dove decided to sleep out again. She, like me, was at home either inside or out, and we wanted our private time. Overall, we spent two days there and they all come to love her as I did. It was sort of a sad day when we left them, but we knew we had some true friends in Pine Ridge and promised to come back for a visit every so often.

Lawassa had to, again, give us big hugs, and held on to Mourning Dove for a good spell. Sarge pumped my hand before pullin' me into a hug and thumpin' my back 'til I saw stars. What a great pair.

Life back in the camp went on as usual; me huntin' and fishin' with the men, learning more and more of the Choctaw language, and spendin' as much time as I could with Mourning Dove. With the help of most of the tribe, we built our own cabin near Owl Feather. I knew he'd miss havin' Mourning Dove around and I wanted her to stay near. We still took our meals with him, since she was the one who cooked for us, and I made sure he had plenty available.

I mostly hunted with John Leaping Deer and a couple of the other braves. One day he asked me, "Why do you call me by my full name?"

"Well, I reckon it's 'cause I never knew just what you like to be called. Some folks like their American name, and some like their Indian name."

"I am Leaping Deer in my thoughts. You may call me whatever you wish, though."

"Honestly, I think of you more as Leaping Deer also. I just didn't want to offend you."

"Jonathon, we are friends, like brothers even. You will not offend me."

"Then Leaping Deer it is, my brother."

"Good, now that is settled. Maybe someday I can teach you how to hunt and you can earn a name, too." He grinned at me, knowin' I thought I was as good a hunter as he was.

One day we come in and there was a lot of hoorah goin' on in the camp. We went on down to where the whole clan was gathered to see what was happenin'. One of the young bucks was layin' on the ground with his right arm all bloody while one of the women was washin' and cleanin' it up for him. You could tell he was in a lot of pain.

It seems he had just got in right before we showed up. He had been out huntin', a long ways out from the camp, when somebody took a shot at him, hittin' him in the arm. He never got a real clear look at them, 'cause he was on horseback, and he lit a shuck out of there.

The only thing he could tell from the brief look he did get was that there was two of them, and they was both large sized men. Bein' they was ridin' too, he had no idea as to how tall they might be.

"I got only a short look at them when I saw movement and looked to see one of them pointing a gun at me," he said. "They could see I was too tall to be game, and they shot anyway. Lucky I saw them first, because I turned my horse at that moment."

"If they shot high enough to hit you in the arm, they were not shooting at game." Leaping Deer opined.

"No, but why would anyone wish to kill me? I had done nothing."

He'd headed to the deep woods then, and hid out in a ravine for a bit, just in case they come lookin' for him. After awhile, not seein' any more of them, he come on home, lickitty-split.

Well, they got him doctored up good, and the men gathered to discuss the happenin's. Nobody could figure why anybody would want to shoot one of them, unless it was for pure meanness. The only thing they figured to do was to send a rider to the fort and let them know what happened, and to warn others to keep a good eye out.

For some reason, my mind turned to the Wiggins boys, Squatty and Ugly, as I called 'em. I don't rightly know why I thought of them, but it sounded like some meanness they'd get up to. Still, maybe I just held ill feelin's for them on account of my own dealin's with 'em. So, I just held my tongue except to tell everybody to be extra careful if they seen two squat men ridin' together, 'cause I'd had trouble with them and didn't think too highly of 'em.

We decided there was not much else we could do. It was doubtful we could find any sign since the brave couldn't really tell us exactly where it happened. He was too busy gettin' to cover to think about that.

The incident weighed on my mind for a while. It didn't make any sense, and I wondered if it weren't them Wiggins for sure. I knew from experience that they were mean enough to kill, even a helpless man.

~ ~ ~ ~ ~

We wintered right well that year. The women had turned out a real good truck patch, and huntin' and fishin' had been good.

It was late spring when Leaping Deer was joshin' me about bein' a lousy hunter when we got back to camp, so we didn't notice, at first, how quiet it was. Not a soul was outside, nor stirrin' about as usual. Suddenly cautious, we brought weapons to hand, and entered camp. Down the way, I seen Owl Feather sittin' outside his cabin door, wrapped in a blanket. When I come up to him, he slowly raised tired old eyes to mine and told me,

"Mourning Dove gone."

Gone? What could he mean? "Tell me," I demanded.

"Shawnee come take her."

I gradually dragged the story from him. She'd been out gathering herbs and berries with Little Fawn and a couple of children, who were playing nearby. Four or five braves had snuck up on them and grabbed the two girls while the kids hid, watchin' in terror. Quickly binding them, the braves had turned away into the trees. After waiting fearfully to make sure the raiders weren't comin' back, the kids ran for the camp and safety.

This had happened yesterday and, all being on the hunt, no men were in camp to pursue. The elders were in no shape to run after the captors through the woods.

Owl Feather had read sign, "Five Shawnee take them. They not ride, but on foot."

"How do you know it was Shawnee?" I asked him.

"Children tell me how they look, what they wear. It was Shawnee. If you find them soon, maybe buy them back. Some Shawnee think it okay to take girls from other tribes. If lucky, they not sell or trade them to others. Must hurry, Jonathon."

"Don't worry, Grandfather, I will leave right now."

My heart was in my throat while fear and anger both battled to control me. Fear for my angel, and anger at the bucks who would so cruelly take her from me. After tellin' me of the signs I must follow, and the general direction of the travel, Owl Feather fetched a pack he'd already made up for me. Hustling to saddle the roan and whistlin' for Rip, I prepared to go after them. Leaping Deer appeared at my side as I rode out and I knew I'd not travel alone.

We found the spot where they captured the girls and followed the trail north by west. With them already over a full day ahead of us, I knowed it might be a long trail, but I was gonna bring back my wife, or die in the tryin'. We made a cold camp that night. Fearful of losing the trail, we didn't try to track 'em in the dark, but was up before dawn broke over the hills. A light rain fell as we continued on our way. This was not good.

The trail meandered a little, but seemed to keep bearin' north and west. I wanted to race ahead, in that direction, but Leaping Deer cautioned against it. Better, he said, to keep on the track and try to make up time, but it pained me sorely not to hurry more. They was on foot and not takin' great pains to hide their trail. At first, we found where one had hung back, or circled around, to look for pursuers. I reckoned they decided nobody was comin' 'cause, pretty soon, they bunched up again.

We was in a huge pine forest when we lost the trail. Ground reining our horses, we backtracked on foot to where we last seen it, and started to search from there. Pine needles, inches thick, littered the ground, and left no place for tracks. If they'd had horses, we mighta' picked up a hoof print, but moccasins left no mark there. Leaping Deer was a better tracker than me, and could track a snake across a pond, but he could find no sign, either. Even Rip had lost the trail due, I reckon, to the rain, the heavy smell of pine, and the passage of time.

As the sun hung low in the sky, I wanted to explode, uproot a tree, fight a bear, or just empty my guns helplessly into the trees. But I didn't. I just kept tryin' to swallow the hard lump in my throat, to ease the pain in my breast, and keep my eyes dry. I wouldn't give up.

Two weeks later, and many miles away, we found what might have been their camp. A Cherokee we'd met two days previous had told us of a Shawnee camp in this area, but said they never stayed long before moving back west. The Shawnee were more of a nomadic tribe than were the Choctaw or Cherokee, and moved about the land assigned to them. Often, they ventured into the lands of the more peaceful tribes, but didn't settle there.

It weren't that all Shawnee were troublesome, but many a white man was crossin' through their lands of late, on the way west, and some of these folks weren't mindful of carin' for the land, or leavin' enough game for the rightful owners. This didn't set well with many of the young bucks who could no longer gain honor as warriors, as was the custom, but had to raid or steal for it.

Many of these bucks wanted to battle the whites, but the elders warned against it, so they'd raid peaceful tribes instead. Later, after gettin' a belly full of bad treatment, they did join up with other angry tribes to attack the folks goin' west, and those that had settled in the area.

Anyway, the camp was gone. There was sign of twelve teepee's, which was good shelter for a nomadic people since they was quick to pack and move. This was a fair sized camp, but not a really big one, and had been pitched near a stream so they could gather plants and catch and dry fish. Many a squaw used fish bones for fine needle work, whereas a quill or even a sharpened piece of seed, with a hole in it, was used for heavy work like buckskin. Smoked fish would make up a good part of their winter diet out on the plains. We tracked the movements of that camp as far as we could.

There came a time when it crossed, and re-crossed, so many other tracks that we just plumb lost it.

Leaping Deer needed to get back and prepare his family for the winter, and I couldn't ask him to stay. He never said it, but I seen the worry in his eyes and his glance often fell towards home. One mornin' as we was breakin' camp, I give him twenty dollars in coin and asked him to buy the necessaries for Owl Feather, and help him get ready for winter.

"Owl Feather respected elder," he told me. "We care for him."

He tried to refuse the money, but I knowed they might need it, and I pushed it on him.

"Go now, good friend," I said, "and care for your family and mine. They need you, and I'll feel better for it."

Part of him wanted to stay and see the job through, but his honor as a provider made him go.

"*Falama Sioshi*', come back my brother," he said. " May the Great Spirit ride with you." He turned and rode away.

"Well, Rip," I says, "It ain't the first time we've done it by ourselves, and I reckon it won't be the last."

The only thing I knew to do was to keep headin' west and hope to find the right camp. This flat country was strange to me, but I knew the Shawnee mostly stayed up in this area in the winter, movin' southeast to hunt and fish in the summer. That much I had learned from Owl Feather.

Chapter 7

DAYS MELTED INTO WEEKS as I rode hundreds of miles back and forth through empty plains in search of my bride, entering camp after camp and talkin' with the people in bits of Choctaw, Shawnee, and English. A few told me they had heard of the two young Choctaw girls, but weren't sure where they might be. I was becoming fearful they'd been sold to another tribe, and might never be found, but I pushed on.

The weather begun to worsen and cold, harsh winds to blow across the endless plains of the northern territories. Days on end were filled with dark clouds scuttling across the skies, darkening the land like swarms of blackbirds.

At one Shawnee camp, I swapped one of my skinnin' knives for a buffalo coat. It was wore some, but mighty warm. That was the same camp where I learned I might be getting near to Mourning Dove and Little Fawn. The elder I'd swapped with admired my way of talking the language so I told him more of my life with the people and of my search for my wife.

Gazing into my eyes, as if to read my spirit, he said, "I have looked into your heart. You are a good man, I think, so I will tell you this. I have heard of the women of which you speak." My heart thumped hard in my chest, like the beat of a huge drum.

"There was a camp, maybe one day's travel to the setting sun. The women were there about a moon ago."

"Thank you, Grandfather, you have made my spirit glad."

"Maybe-so they are still there," he grunted, "maybe not. But your search is good, and I hope you find your bride."

Saying goodbye, and thanks, to the old man, I pulled out
and headed west. The next mornin', I saw the village in the
distance.

Like I said, the Shawnee was mostly good, friendly folks
but some of the young bucks were set on mischief, and the
constant encroachment on and through their lands was caus-
ing some ill will. Just to be on the safe side, I figured to up
my odds of a welcome; I dressed in my white wedding buckskins, and wore my finest moccasins.

After shavin', and braiding my long, black hair, I pulled
my medicine bag around my neck, to let it hang in front. I
also braided the roan's tail and mane. You never knew what
might impress an Indian. Sitting tall and straight in my saddle, I rode slowly and calmly into the Shawnee village,
lookin' only straight ahead, until I came to a stop in front of
the meetin' lodge. There stood a lone warrior, not dressed
any special way, but you could tell he was somebody important, just by the way he stood.

Neither of us spoke or moved for what seemed like a
long time, just took each other's measure. I don't know what
he saw, but I saw the pride of hundreds of years lookin' out
at me.

"Ya-ta-hay." I greeted him in the language of the plains.

"Ya-ta-hay." He replied and raised his open palm to me.

The open palm was a sign of peace, indicating no
weapon was held. It's kinda how shakin' hands got started,
but most Indians don't care to touch strangers, so shakin'
hands was hard for them, and unnatural. He motioned me
down, and I could tell he was impressed with the way I
dressed and rode so calmly into his village, but he tried not
to show it.

After goin' through the usual ceremony that came with
such a visit, we finally got down to business. I learned he
was a leader among his people, and he learned of my living
with the Choctaw. We knew enough of each other's language to get by. Finally, I got around to tellin' him of
Mourning Dove and Little Fawn. I spoke long of my search
for them and how much I needed to find my wife, to buy

them back if necessary. I also told him I'd heard they might be here, in this camp.

By this time, a small crowd had gathered and I saw, out the corner of my eye, a young brave dart a glance at another before they both looked quickly away. Nothin' was said, but I noticed a shift in the leader's eyes. He told me no, the girls were not in his camp, and I believed him. No way would he lie to me, another *nakni tushka,* (warrior), but he also wouldn't feel it necessary to tell me the whole truth.

I had a strong suspicion the girls had at least been here, and I could have asked him outright, but that would have put him in a bad spot, and I couldn't do that. My fears were realized, though, that the girls had been swapped again, and were likely far, far away.

I did ask if he had any idea where they might be, or if he could help me find them. He just told me no, that he did not know where they were and, again, I believed him. It's likely he did not know their whereabouts, but still wasn't telling me the whole story. We spoke of other things for a while, and then I said goodbye and left them in peace. I felt like just breakin' down, but no way could I show any emotion before that honorable man.

~ ~ ~ ~ ~

The first blizzard of the season struck that night. Not long past day's end, that cruel wind begun to howl like a pack of wolves, and the cold cut me deep, even with that coat. Soon, I begun to feel the sting of ice like bees on my face where I weren't covered, and the cold got worse.

"Rip," I says to him, "we're in bad trouble if we don't find shelter. Trouble is, there ain't much out on these plains."

I tugged the coat collar up as close as I could around my ears and cheeks, pulled my hat down to protect my eyes, and prodded the roan on westward. I felt him quiver as, head down, he plodded on. Ol' Rip tucked in close to us and we kept huntin' a likely spot.

Pretty soon, the ground was covered with a blanket of ice and snow mix that made crunchin' sounds under the roan's hoofs. We was all getting' pretty miserable when I spotted a crack in the blanket of ice and, nudgin' Horse that way with my knees, come upon a deep ditch cuttin' through the land like a jagged scar. It was about twelve foot wide and six or eight foot deep, and looked mighty good right then. Easin' along the edge, I finally found a spot where, dismounted, I got me and the horse down in that gully.

Just bein' out of that wind was a relief, but I knowed we'd need more. Bein' in a wash, it didn't take me long to gather enough kindlin' wood to start a fire against the bank, where the heat would reflect more. Once it was goin' I searched up and down the gully for more wood, and piled up a good supply, then unsaddled the roan and rubbed some of the ice off him with his blanket. He stood, head down, as close to the fire as he dared.

Wrappin' the coat tight around me I stretched my legs out near the fire, added a few more sticks, and leaned back agin' the cut bank. Rip crawled closer to my outstretched legs and settled down with a shiver. Bein' as he was short-haired, I know that wind must of cut right through him. We weren't exactly comfortable, but it was some better than a short while back, and we settled in for a cold night. That storm lasted for three days.

Sometime later, I woke to find the fire was down to coals. Just as I started to build it back up, I saw Rip's ears come up and heard a low growl. His head came off my leg, to test the air, but I doubted he could smell anything in that wind. I did, though, figure he heard something, and I trusted his instincts.

Instead of adding wood, I kicked a little snow over the fire to kill even the small glow. Layin' a hand on Rip's neck to quiet him, I waited, strainin' to see into that white blanket of driven snow. I could feel Rip's muscles tighten and the low rumble in his throat, but I couldn't see ten feet in that whiteout. I knew anybody, or anything, out in that storm was either lost, crazy, or up to no good.

I figured if I moved around I'd likely be seen but I had to know what was about. Since I hadn't had a chance to change outta' my white outfit, I shed the buffalo coat and slipped into the storm wearin' nothin' but my white buckskins. Stayin' low, I scooted up that gully a ways before stickin' my head up. Seeing nothing, I eased out of the ditch and slowly made my way toward where Rip had been starin'.

Suddenly, in the midst of the blizzard, I sensed movement. Frozen in place, I strained to make it out. I barely saw what at first appeared to be two bears, walkin' upright, stalkin' my camp. My mind was frazzled from the howling of the storm, but I knowed that couldn't be right. Then, I realized it was two bundled up people, covered in snow.

Starting to call out to them, thinkin' they must be in trouble, I decided to hold my tongue. As they crept closer, and I noticed how furtively they were movin', I knew the truth. It was the two braves from the camp. They must have followed me, hangin' back far enough to not be seen. With the storm coming up, and tryin' to stay warm, I hadn't checked my back-trail much. The glow of my fire must have give them a direction.

Not wanting to shoot any innocent people, I pulled my knife and waited some more. The wind briefly parted the curtain of snow, and my eyes met those of the closest one. It was one of the braves, for sure. About then, unable to stand the strain of worryin' about me I guess, Rip come tearin' out of nowhere and leaped astraddle of the one farthest from me. I couldn't let him get hurt fightin' for me, so I tackled the other, only to find him also armed with a knife.

Instinctively grabbin' his knife hand, I jerked him towards me. It was a struggle to keep his blade away from my chest, and it became a battle of strength. Lean I might be, after all my wanderin', and my wounds, but I was still strong.

Now I never wanted to hurt or kill anybody, but a man has to protect himself and what's his. Me and him tussled a bit, his knife coming too close to my face, before I felt my blade go into his side. He held me tight for another moment then, with a sigh, sunk to the ground. I could only stand there on tremblin' legs as the full impact of what happened hit me broadside.

Barely able to stand, I went to where Rip had the other brave pinned to the snow. He was curled up tight, tryin' to protect himself, when I called Rip off him. Bein' real careful, I rolled him onto his back while Rip controlled him with low growls and the meanest look you ever saw.

His eyes were wide with fright and I weren't sure he was breathin' until I got closer to his face. I know Rip, appearin' out of nowhere like that, had scared him good. And me, standin' there in nothing but a white suit, covered in snow, with a bloody knife in my hand, musta' been a sight from hell.

I leaned close to his ear and, in Choctaw, said, "Tell me now about the girls." He began right away to babble his story.

It seems him and some other young bucks had taken a trip to check out the area southeast of them, and see what they might find to steal. They had come upon Mourning Dove and Little Fawn and, without really thinkin' it out, grabbed the girls and ran.

He swore neither of the girls had been mistreated or harmed in any way. They got word somebody was huntin' for them and, since neither girl would have anything to do with any brave in the camp, they figured the safest thing was to sell or trade them to another camp.

It turned out there was a group of Cheyenne camping to the west, so they taken them there, to be traded as camp slaves. Both girls was okay when they left 'em, but the Cheyenne soon departed for their winter lands far to the northwest. His leader told the truth; they had no idea where this camp might be, and he was awful sorry about the girls.

About then, he started to plead for his life. He begged the "Spirit Warrior" not to take him and swore to be a friend. He was babblin' about the giant wolf demon who fought with the Spirit Warrior and I realized he was talkin' about me and Rip.

While he kept runnin' on, I was thinking. Before I let him up, I told Rip, in English, to "Find Horse." He made sure I was okay, then he turned back into the gully and out of sight.

Right then, I commenced to singing a war chant, makin' it up as I went along. I sang of the great demon wolf, and of the Spirit Warrior's search for his bride. I sang that any who harmed her would be forever followed and haunted by the two until they drug him into the fire pits of the demon world. His eyes got bigger and bigger as he took it in.

Finally, I told him, "Take the body of your friend, and go from here. Treat him in the way of the warrior, so that his spirit may come and ride with me and the demon wolf. He would wish to aid in our quest."

As soon as he was out of sight, I rushed right to my fire and built it up as big as I could stand it. After warming the inside of my coat over the flames, I pulled it on before sinking down to the ground. Lord, to be warm again!

It bothered me a lot to have taken that young buck's life, but he brung the fight to me. Had they left me be, I'd have just kept lookin' for the girls, and never bothered them. I reckon they thought I might come huntin' them, so they decided to take me down first. On the plus side, I figured I'd be safer after the story of the Spirit Warrior and his wolf got around.

~ ~ ~ ~ ~

The silence woke me. After three days of howling winds, it didn't seem right somehow. Shakin' the snow from my coat, I climbed up the bank to stare at a strange, silent land. Nothin' but low mounds, like lumps under a quilt, broke the cover of whiteness stretchin' as far as I could see. Here and there a snow covered tree or bush broke the emptiness but, to a hill boy, it was the most awesome thing I ever remembered seein'. Not a creature was stirrin' on the ground. Far away, I seen a hawk circlin' high overhead, lookin' for his first meal in days.

I stood there a long while, eyes squinted against the glare, just enjoyin' the sun beamin' down on the brilliant sea of white, and the wonderful absence of that howling wind, before droppin' back into the gully to get ready for travel. We still had a job ahead of us.

That was a hard winter on us. We roamed when we could, avoiding any Indians we seen outside their camps, and I wore my finery whenever I entered one. It may seem strange to us, but most Indians that would hunt down and kill a man outside their camp will let you be if you ride right in. It's just they have a different way of lookin' at things, and admire courage in any man. While in their camp or village, you were as safe as in your own bed but, outside of it, you were fair game if they was on the path.

Nearly every camp had heard the story of the two young Choctaw girls, but nobody knew for sure where they might be. I soon began to get a different notice when I rode in wearing my white buckskins. Some people went inside and pulled the cover over their doorway, and others seemed to stay as far away from me as possible, lookin' around them fearfully. I figured they had by now heard of the Spirit Warrior and his demon wolf, and was checkin' for Rip.

Rip, of course, never entered a camp with me; he had just rather stay out and roam around the area. Once in a while, somebody would get a glimpse of him at a distance, and his size only added to the story.

Before long, me, Horse, and Rip was all getting' mighty pore. Our ribs was stickin' out and we looked pretty rough except when I gusssied up to visit. We were getting' awful tired, too, and I gave some thought to going back to the village and talking with Owl Feather. Odds were, the Cheyenne would not be back before late spring, if then.

We took a couple of days to lay up and fatten up. I found a good spot to camp where I could hunt and fish, and where Horse could nibble the tender bark from some smaller trees. The only things I missed was salt and coffee. While we was restin' up, I did a lot of studyin' on our situation.

Come spring, this country was gonna fill up with huntin' and raidin' parties and I didn't know how long we could avoid them. Also, I figured I needed to take some word back to the folks about what happened to the girls. I knew they was all wonderin' about us, and Owl Feather might be needin' my help with somethin'.

Though I hated to leave without finding the girls, I decided to head back home for a while and see if Leaping Deer wanted to come back with me later.

It was a long, lonesome ride back to the place I now called home, and I gotta' admit I wasn't proud to be comin' back alone. I knew they'd all be glad to see me, but they'd still be mournin' in camp.

Two days out from the camp, I spotted a lone rider and, after studyin' him awhile, I saw it was Leaping Deer. His greeting was joyous, but forlorn at the same time. He said they'd given us all up for dead or lost, and he felt he needed to go to try to find us, or learn our fate if possible We just stayed there that whole day talkin' about everything. I learned how the camp had fared and that Owl Feather was doin fine. As I was tellin' Leaping Deer of my travels, the fight and all, he suddenly leaped to his feet.

"Waagh," he shouted, "Even here we've heard of the Spirit Warrior who keeps a demon wolf at his side! This is you?"

In his delight at the tale of the war chant, and the brave's fright, he danced around me and started shouting, "Spirit Warrior, Spirit Warrior!" over and over as he laughed out loud.

I knew this was a story to bring joy to the hearts of my people, but which would never be shared outside our own circle. Let others beware the Spirit Warrior and his demon wolf.

The next couple of weeks were hard on me. I moped around, hunted and fished, and spent hours just sittin' with Owl Feather and starin' into the woods. We also talked on and on, and he kept tellin' me that, no matter how much it hurt us, the land was far to big for me to hold out hope of finding Mourning Dove.

"You gave your best," He said," And if we could have found them sooner, there was a chance."

"The lands of the Cheyenne, and others, reach to the far mountains, far too vast for even a whole tribe to search; you must now think of other things."

It broke my heart to hear it, but I knew it to be true. The problem was, without Mourning Dove I felt lost, even here among friends. Living here would be a nightmare for me, I knew. Memories of Mourning Dove were everywhere I looked, so I talked more with Owl Feather about my thoughts.

The Texas Rangers seemed to be callin' me. I knew about them only what I'd heard, and didn't even know if they'd take me, but that's where my mind kept goin'. I knew they were the only law in some wild country, and that they had a reputation for being hard but fair, so it seemed like the sort of life that might appeal to me since I'd lost Mourning Dove. I just knew I couldn't stay here, as much as I cared for these fine people. Owl Feather understood, and so did Leaping Deer and the others.

Christmas was nigh, and the thought of being here, without my bride, made every beat of my heart become a thud of despair. I just couldn't face it, and knew not what to do. Confusion wrapped itself tightly around my thoughts, as if to comfort the pain there.

I made a trip down to see Sarge and Lawassa, I guess to say good-bye. With the Texas Rangers back on my mind and, without the family I'd dreamed of to keep me here, I figured to see if I couldn't join up. I'd already said my good-bye's to the people and, except for a few dollars, left my poke with Leaping Deer. He again tried to refuse it, but I insisted it was for Owl Feather.

"Save it if you must, but I'll feel better if it's here for him. I have more hides to sell."

Finally, he relented.

Me and Sarge yarned for a couple of days, he bought what pelts I had brought, and I fattened up some more on Lawassa's good cookin'. They mourned with me the loss of Mourning Dove and laughed with me about the tale of the Spirit Warrior, after promising never to repeat it.

Sayin' bye to them was as hard as leaving my other friends, and I promised I'd try to come back to visit. It's a good bet that I was a sorry sight ridin' out of there with Rip tailin' along behind.

Chapter 8

I FIGURED TO CROSS the Red River south of Fort Towson and find my way to the Ranger headquarters near Waco. My plan was to stop at the fort and pick up the few things Sarge didn't have, but that I'd need for a long ride.

Fort Towson wasn't a fort in the common sense. It didn't have high walls for protection and such; it was just a group of buildings laid out in a pattern with barracks and other buildings down each side and the headquarters buildin' at the end, with a parade ground in front of it. It was built in 1824 to guard the Spanish border, but was closed and then re-opened later to serve and protect the people of the Choctaw tribe.

I came up to the fort near sundown, and decided to stop in at the café in the nearby town for some grub. There was a couple of soldiers jawin' with the man runnin' the place, but otherwise I had it to myself. I ordered up a plate of beef stew, cornbread, and some apple pie with coffee. I'd just started in on my fourth cup of coffee and a big slab of apple pie when the door opened and who should walk in but the Wiggins brothers, Ugly and Squatty. I decided to just ignore them and finish my meal, but they wasn't gonna allow it.

"Well, looky who's here," Squatty piped up, "That sorry Stout runt. We figured you'd left the country."

Without lookin' up from my pie, I said, "Least I ain't never tried to murder anybody. Especially when they was lyin' helpless."

I spoke loud enough for them to hear, and that got the attention of the others, too. It got real quiet for a minute, then Squatty spoke up again.

"What are you tryin' to say, Stout," He demanded.

"Tryin' ain't the word," I answered, "I said it plain enough. You and your brother bushwhacked me one night and, if it hadn't been for my dog, was gonna kill me while I lay helpless on the ground. You denyin' it?"

"Hell, yeah!" He snarled, "And I'm gonna make you regret them words. Get your iron, and get outside."

"Why?" I asked, "So your brother can backshoot me while I'm watchin' you? That's the way you two work, ain't it?"

Oh, that made him mad, all right. He huddled with his brother for a minute and I looked over at them soldier boys. One of them picked up his carbine that had been leanin' against the wall, and returned my look flatly.

Squatty swung back towards me and started to say somethin' else, but I'd had enough.

"Sir," I spoke to the soldier with the carbine, "If you'd kindly make sure they stay inside 'til I've got my pistol, I'd appreciate it."

"No problem," he replied, lifting the barrel toward them while his friend gathered up his own gun.

"I'll be just a minute," I said, then stepped out to my horse. I didn't go around armed in cafes and such, 'cause it really weren't necessary. Usually, that is. Now, I was beginnin' to think I should start.

When I'd got my rig, and was strappin' it on, I walked over to the Wiggins brothers' horses. I didn't know who rode which, but one of 'em had a kicked out left back hoof. That pretty well summed things up for me, and I felt that swarm of angry bees in my head again.

This trash had more than likely killed my Paw, and burned my cabin. I knew for sure that they had bushwhacked me and would have killed me in cold blood if Rip hadn't flew into them like he did. It was time we settled up. I stepped into the middle of the street and checked my loads. Puttin' the Colt back loosely into the holster I'd made special for it, I called out to them inside.

"Ya'll can let 'em come out now."

Steppin' to the door, one of the soldier boys asked, "Don't you want us to keep the other one in here, or keep him covered so he don't get in this?"

"Nope, send 'em both out, and step out of the way."

He looked at me like I was crazy, but done as I said. I was ready this time, in case they tried to get the jump on me, like before, but they both come out and split apart about ten feet. I guess they was scared to come out shootin', because of them soldiers. The soldiers, and the owner, stood at a window off to the side, and watched us.

I waited, feet spread and balanced, hand near my gun butt, as they looked at each other for some signal. I know they figured they had me, two against one, and it may have been foolish of me to take 'em both on like this, but I wanted this to end here and now. One, two, or all of us was gonna end this day face down in the dirt. What with all that I had suffered at their hands, and the pain of losin' my angel, my wife, I really didn't care how it ended. That was my edge; I just didn't care.

Knowin' Squatty for the sneak he was, I watched him, but kept the other in my vision too. I couldn't let them get further apart, and I knew it, or they'd have me. Lucky for me, they wasn't smart enough to spread out more.

Squatty tried to draw my attention off him by sneakin' a look toward his brother. That's when his hand grabbed for his gun, and his brother was right behind.

That long barrel pistol just jumped into my hand. Thanks to the holster, I didn't have to lift it the full 9 inches, and it come up in the blink of an eye. Squatty hadn't cleared leather when the roar of exploded powder shattered the stillness, and that gun bucked in my fist. I put another into Squatty, to make sure he went down, before I turned the Colt on his brother.

The sound of his gun erupting, and the puff of dust at my feet told it all. He was scared, and tried too hard to beat me; he missed with his first shot, and that's all he got.

Twice more my Colt spoke, and both times I saw the shock of those bullets hittin' his chest. He stayed on his feet for a moment, then he tumbled into the dirt to join his brother. It was over.

It didn't take long for a crowd to gather, drawn by the gunfire. The soldiers told everybody what had happened, and swore it was self-defense, so I weren't worried about the law huntin' me.

People told me them boys, the brothers, had been raisin' cane around these parts for a long while, and had beat one poor soldier near to death. The law couldn't touch 'em, though, 'cause they goaded him into swingin' first. Really, they seemed proud I'd put 'em down, like they was mad dogs or something. I guess, in a way, they was.

It didn't take long for the word to get around how I had shucked that pistol in a blink and put two bullets into Squatty before either of them got off a shot. I didn't want no reputation as a gunslinger, so I played that down as how slow they was, but them soldier boys kept on talkin' it up.

The fort Commander showed up and, after listenin' to the witnesses, had a hearing right on the spot. He declared it self-defense, and said he'd write up a report that way, so I was clear to go.

Everybody wanted to buy me drinks but, not bein' much in the mood for liquor, I told them I'd have one with 'em, but that I had a hard ride ahead of me and couldn't have more. They seemed disappointed until I toasted Fort Towson, and the Army, then told 'em to buy each other drinks on my behalf. That seemed to satisfy them, and they all smiled and shook my hand.

To me, a killin', no matter how low the snake, weren't nothin' to celebrate, but some folks feel different I guess. I don't mean to say I felt bad, just not like celebratin'. Them boys had tried to kill me and it was likely they had killed my paw. There weren't no sorrow at their passin', but they was still livin' men, and somebody's sons, so I weren't proud of what I had to do.

It was getting' late when the commander said he'd see to their buryin', and bid me goodnight. I eased out the door while everybody was still a jawin' about the fight, and tightened the cinch on Horse before mountin' up and whistlin' for Rip. He come around the corner of the building and, givin' me his "about time" look, trotted off down the road ahead of me. I figured to camp tonight in Texas.

It wasn't but a few more miles to the river crossin', so we eased on down that way just takin' it easy. I reflected on what all had happened since the day Paw's horse come home without him, and how happy I'd been while courtin', and winnin', Mourning Dove.

Her absence left a big hole in my heart that I knew would never be filled just the same way again. I also thought of my friends in the Nation—of Owl Feather, Leaping Deer, Sarge, Lawassa, and the others. I knew I'd miss them, but sometimes a man's destiny leads him away from the comfort of one place, to the unknown of another.

My search for the girls came to mind, and how close I had come to finding them, only to lose the trail. Unbidden, and unwanted, a tear sprang to my eye at this thought, just as I spied the river ahead. I pushed the roan into the red water of that crossing, shallow and wide here, and splashed across with Rip at my side.

"Well, boys." I said, "I reckon we're Texans now."

It was getting well into the night, so I just wanted to bed down 'til morning. Finding a good spot under the spreading limbs of a towering oak, I gathered a few small sticks for morning coffee, and then slipped into my bedroll.

A million thoughts swarmed my mind, chief among them being Mourning Dove and Little Fawn. What was their fate? Where were they, and how were they doing? Had they, by now, taken one of the braves for a husband?

These things, and others, kept me awake for a while, but tiredness finally pulled me into a restless sleep.

Chapter 9

IN THE CHILL GRAYNESS of predawn, I slipped from my bed and started the fire. It was too small to do much more then brew up some coffee, but I figured to eat later. Holding my hands near the warmth, I inhaled the brisk tang of wood smoke, and waited for the coffee to heat. There's nothin' better than the smell of fresh coffee brewin' over a wood fire. Grabbing a couple of cold biscuits from my saddlebags, I tossed one to Rip, and slowly chewed on the other while considering my situation.

Could I ever be satisfied without finding the truth of what happened to Mourning Dove? I know Owl Feather figured he told me the right thing when he said I would likely never find her, but could I abandon her to her fate? My heart and mind were so torn with indecision that I just couldn't think. For now, I'd go on into Texas. If I still couldn't accept her loss, I'd have to find some way of trying again. There seemed to be no clear answer.

After making sure the fire was totally dead, I tossed the blanket and saddle on the roan and tightened the cinches. He seldom got frisky, but the crisp air of the morning and a night's rest had him actin' foolish today. He kept movin' away from me every time I tried to hook the stirrup, and crow-hopped a bit just to show me he was feelin' his oats.

When I finally pulled his head down and got my foot settled, I swung my right leg up and over his rump. Just as my butt hit the seat, that idiot horse decided he was a two-year old colt again, and went to jayhawkin' it all over the clearing, with me hanging on for dear life.

Now, I never claimed to be no cowboy, so I hung on to that saddle horn like a starvin' man holding onto a chicken leg. Maybe that wasn't the cowboy way, but there was no glory in bein' tossed on your behind by a pea-brained horse. Especially since nobody was watchin'.

Once he settled down, I smacked him lightly beside his head and said, "I hope you got all that out of your system, you bag of horse droppin's. Much more, and I'll trade you for a mule."

There were two towns in easy riding distance of where we camped. To the east, there was Clarksville, and southwest was the town of Paris. Since we was headed southwest, Paris it would be.

This part of Texas was sure nice country, kinda like the lower part of the Nations—rolling hills and a bevy of different trees. We rode through Bois D'arc, Oak, native Pecan, Hickory, and wild Plum, with a scattering of big Cedars thrown in.

From where I'd crossed the Red, it was only about ten miles to Paris and it was a nice comfortable ride. This area was pretty well settled, and I saw scattered cabins here and there. Prior to 1830, there had been some Indian raids in this area, with the worst bein' when a party of braves attacked a small settlement, killing a bunch of women, kids, and slaves. The menfolk had been out huntin', and found their families' bodies upon their return.

Bein' mad as all get-out, they took off after the Indians, but came near to bein' wiped out them selves. Only a couple of them survived to tell about it. A man named Emberson had settled nearby in 1824, and he told of raids after that, but no major killin's that I knowed of.

With the increase in population, this area was safe now, but in other parts of Texas people still slept under a blanket of fear due to raiding Apache and Comanche.

Ridin' into town, I saw a brickyard and a sawmill in operation, so it was no real surprise to see several brick buildings in town. It was something of a surprise, though, to see how big the town was. There were schools, churches, a courthouse, and a thriving downtown square. Except for Fort Smith, this was the biggest town I'd been in, and it felt a little strange to a country boy like me. I reckoned I'd best get used to it, though, 'cause Austin and Waco was surely bigger.

Unless I called him in, Rip always stayed outside of camps or towns I visited. He'd rather roam the neighborhood on his own than be underfoot and around a bunch of people, so I usually let him decide. He always found me, so I didn't fret him getting lost, and he was too smart to get into any trouble with people. He knew the difference between free game and folk's livestock or pets.

Looping my reins at the hitchin' rail, I patted the roan's neck and stepped up onto the boardwalk. This was another example of a growing community, real boardwalks to keep your feet out of the mud and horse droppin's so common in most small settlements. Seems like they kept this town pretty well cleaned up too, 'cause there was a couple of men, with a cart and shovels, workin' hard at keepin' the street clean. You didn't see that everywhere.

Now everybody knows the best place in any town to get news, travel tips, or gossip, and to make deals, is in the saloon. So, that's where I headed first. Besides, it was getting' near lunch time and most saloons offered some kind of free eats, which I was ready for.

Inside, it was smoky and dim. A couple of lanterns cast the only light other than the two big windows in the front, and most of the customers seemed to be smokin' somethin', whether it be a cigar, pipe, or a hand-rolled cigarette.

To the left of the door were a few round tables, with a couple of folks playin' a listless game of penny poker at one of them. Along the bar that stretched from the front to near the back, on my right, stood five men in various dress. A couple was surely farmers, wearin' clodhopper boots and over-hauls with a bib front.

The rest appeared to be city men, dressed in waistcoats and full shirts. One wore a coat and a white shirt, with his black trousers stuffed into some real sharp lookin' hand-tooled boots. He appeared to be in his twenties, with a look of prosperity about him. It was him that I chose to step up beside as I ordered up a beer.

The first sip was pure pleasure. It was cold, and slid easily down my parched throat.

"I never expected such cold beer," I told the bartender.

"Yep, got us a real ice house out west of town a mite. We keep the beer kegs in the back room with ice, and run the tap through the wall here. Our customers shore seem to appreciate it on a hot day."

The sharp dressed fellow had just finished his beer, and I offered him another.

"Don't know why not." He turned toward me as he spoke.

"Sam Maxey," he offered his hand.

"A pleasure, Mister Maxey. Jonathon Stout, recently of the Indian Territories."

"Salute, Mister Stout." He lifted his fresh beer. "What brings you to our fair city, if I may inquire?"

"Of course, Sir. I'm passin' through on my way south. My hope is to sign up with your Texas Rangers, if they'll have me, and please call me Jon."

"My pleasure, Sir, and I am Sam to my friends, new and old." He looked me up and down, taking in my 6' 1" height, my beaded buckskin shirt, and the moccasins on my feet. His gaze stopped momentarily at the Colt on my hip, tucked into my homemade holster.

"If you can use that iron, Jon, they will probably accept you eagerly. The footwear, though, may need changing. Men who ride in west and south Texas need tall boots, into which they tuck their trousers. It's more for protection from the mesquite and chaparral through which they ride than for looks. Sometimes it seems everything out there is meant to claw, scratch, or puncture you."

"Reckon I'll need to get me some then. These were most handy where I've been ridin', though. Guess I can save 'em for another time, when they may be better suited."

"You seem to know whereof you speak, Sir," I continued, "Did you perhaps ride with the Rangers?"

"Oh no, but I did ride in the recent Mexican conflict, after I graduated from West Point, and I was in on the capture of the City of Mexico. I just decided a military career was not for me, and now practice law here in Paris."

He seemed awful young for all of that, but when I reflected on my age, and experiences, I realized how young we all were when we assumed the role of men in this country. Age didn't seem nearly as important as the cut of a man's cloth.

"Would you care to sup with my family tonight, Jon, and perhaps stay the night?"

"I'm mightily obliged, Sam, but I have a friend, by name of Rip, waiting for me, and I planned on making a few more miles before we camp."

I explained who Rip was, and he replied, "Ahh, I see. Well, another time, perhaps. It has been a real pleasure making your acquaintance, Jon. Please stop again if you are through this area, and feel free to call on me if you ever need my assistance."

"The same to you, Sam. If all Texans are as kind as you, I'll truly enjoy it here."

Going back to the roan, I rode him down to the livery where I had the hostler bring him a bag of oats to eat while I unsaddled and rubbed him down good. After he got a big drink of fresh water, and was again saddled up, we rode on out of Paris, with me reflecting on my chance encounter with Sam Maxey. It was men like him who would build this country into a civilized nation. I hoped to do my part, too. As we rode out of town, Rip appeared from the surrounding woods and give me his look again.

"Well," I told him, "You could have come in with us, but you decided to chase rabbits instead, so don't gripe at me."

How he always seemed able to find me, wherever I rode out, was still a mystery to me. Maybe we was just so close that he knew my mind like I did. Reckon I'll never figure it out.

Sam had told me of the best place to cross the nearby Sulphur River, and the best route to Waco from here. He'd also talked of how the Rangers had come about.

In the earlier days of Texas history, parts of Texas just couldn't be settled. Aside from the Apache from the southwest, and the Mexicans, the Comanche raided as far down as the coast. There were also bandits, just purely bad men, who would take whatever they wanted from people, and often took their lives, too.

The young government saw a need for a group of men who could 'range' about the country, going wherever the need was most obvious, and doing it quickly. They found a few good men and made them Captains of the 'Rangers', and these men recruited their own forces with the promise of action, deprivation, and low—or no—pay. Surprisingly, they found them.

Some of these men became natural leaders, men who lead from the front, not behind the lines. Although the Rangers were tough, and often undisciplined, they were kept honest and soon earned the respect of all the folks who settled the Republic of Texas.

They proved themselves capable, courageous, and ready to tackle any and all who threatened the peace. Never running from a fight, they instead searched them out, and were not afraid of long odds. This made them a force to be reckoned with.

~ ~ ~ ~ ~

It was a long hard ride from the Nations to Waco. I never reckoned on how big Texas really was, and I'd only ridden a small part of it. With no reason to linger, I rode pretty much straight through, stoppin' only to hear more talk, or buy a few supplies.

Much of the talk in the saloons was of the current rash of Indian trepidations out west, and how the United States government seemed unable to do anything about the situation. Chewin' the fat with local farmers, ranchers, and townspeople, I heard many a disgruntled remark. Some said as how they wondered if Texas had done the wrong thing by joining the union, and talked of maybe withdrawing from it.

Rumor had it that Captain Ford had been authorized to set up another Ranger battalion to try and clear the Comanche from west Texas. That news fit right into my plans, and I hoped to catch him before he got a full count. The news was that he was in Austin, but would be headed to Waco soon. Waco was a good-sized town, so I told Rip to come on in with me 'cause I had no idea how long I'd be there. He was good at caring for himself, but I took no chances if I had any doubts. He could bunk in the stable with the roan. Horse was in good shape, considerin' the miles we'd made, but I took him to the livery barn anyway.

"Rub him down good and give him a bait of corn and oats," I told the livery boy.

"Yes, Sir!" He said with a big grin at the two bits I tossed him. I weren't rich, but a hard-workin' boy, with a grin like that, was worth two bits anytime. I grabbed my saddlebags and left him to it.

Rip stayed at my heels as I walked around admiring the town and lookin' for a boarding house or hotel. A bath was first on my list, as one was needed in the worst way. The braided hair down my back was another thing that concerned me, as I didn't know the Rangers' code on such things. I was to learn that Rip Ford didn't care if you wore it past your behind as long as it didn't interfere with your shootin'.

Spying a bathhouse and barbershop, I meandered on in, leavin' Rip outside the door. The barbershop was in front, with two barber chairs bein' occupied and a full bench along the other wall. A man of about forty held a leather strop in one hand and was sharpening a razor on it. A grizzled old timer was cuttin' hair behind the other chair, and it was he who spoke, "You be wantin' a bath, it's four bits—and another four fer a haircut and shave."

"Dang," I thought, "That's a dollar total. If I don't get on with the Rangers, I'll have to find some work."

"Good enough," I said, "I'll take the lot."

"The bath is through that back door," he pointed. "Tell old Sam I said to fix you up. Have him holler when you get done, and I'll save you a chair."

"'Preciate it." I stepped through the door into a hallway with numbered doors off to each side, like a hotel. At the end of the hall was a man who appeared older than dirt, and about as clean. Sweat began to trickle down my back from the heat of the big wood-fired stove in back.

"If ye be wantin' a bath, grab room number two there," he shouted. "I'll be right in with more hot water in a minute."

Inside the room was a tin washtub about four feet long by two feet wide, with water up near a third of the way. Testin' with my fingers, I found it warm so begun to shuck my clothes. From the saddlebags came a fresh shirt, clean underwear, and buckskin britches. These were hung up on some nails driven into the walls, where I hoped the heat and moisture in the room might get some of the wrinkles out.

I only had one more buckskin shirt and a pair of homespun britches to my name, but that was more than some folks had. I'd ask Sam about gettin' my dirty ones washed. Pullin' the solitary chair over by the tub, I laid my pistol and belt on it so it'd be near at hand. Since my run-in with the Wiggins', I kept it a little closer than before. Takin' off my hat last, I stepped into that warm tub.

Oh Lordy, that bath felt good. Sam appeared and poured a big bucket of hot water into it, makin' it just this side of intolerable, which was perfect. Sinkin' into it as far as I could, I felt it just pull the tiredness from my muscles and bones.

After twenty minutes or so of just layin' there, I took up the brush and a bar of lye soap and commenced to scrubbin'. Soon, old Sam came back with another full bucket that he poured right over my head, rinsin' all the soap and grime off. I felt like a new man.

After finishing up the bath, shave, and a haircut, the saloon was, naturally, the next stop. Here in Waco, too, a lot of the talk was about the Indians, how bad the army was, and what was gonna be done about it. They all had heard about Governor Runnels giving Captain Ford authority to set up another company of Rangers, and spoke highly of the idea.

"Well, it's about time they done somethin'," said one young man, "the army ain't worth the cost of their boots."

"Now hold on," cautioned another, "The army cain't do nothin' the government don't want done. You cain't blame the soldier boys; it's the government what keeps 'em under wraps."

After some more of this talkin' back and forth, I struck up a conversation with a feller wearin' a constable's badge.

"I heard Captain Ford was in town," I said, "and was hopin' to join up with him."

"You look a mite young," he opined, "but Cap'n Ford needs young, tough men. He might take you on, but not if yore just lookin' to use that shootin' iron."

"Well Sir, it has seen some use, but I'm not a shootist, if that's what you mean."

Oh, he don't want no gunslingers, but reliable men who can fight and still follow direction. Men with a cool head and lots of grit; some of the so-called minute men that wants to be Rangers ain't worth their salt. I heered he was gonna get rid of some of them and get the Rangers back on track. I shore hope so."

Figuring it was time for some grub, and needing to check my animals, I found out where the Captain was stayin' and headed out the door.

Just as the door closed behind me, I heard, "I ought to kick that damn dog off the walk."

"That's probably not a good idea." I said to a drunken cowboy who was lookin' down at Rip.

"And why the hell not?" He slurred his words.

"I reckon it's 'cause he'll tear your leg off if you try. Besides, my paw taught me not to mistreat animals, and my dog takes offense at people bein' stupid."

"I suppose you're sayin' I'm stupid?" He puffed up his chest, tryin' to impress both me and his equally wobbly friend.

"Nope. Not yet. Only if you try to kick that wolf dog there."

Rip seemed to realize he was the object of our little talk, and raised his head from his paws, his ears cocked as if waiting for a word from me. Not wantin' to start my time in town with a fight, and really not wantin' Rip to eat this man's leg, I led the cowboy down an easier path.

"Rip," I says, "Smile for the man, show him you're friendly." Now Rip had learned to smile a long time ago, so he peeled back his lips, opened his mouth a bit, and showed about an acre of long, sharp teeth.

"See Mister, he's right friendly if you leave him be, but be real careful of makin' him mad. Why, he got that tore up ear from tackling a bear that ate some of his food. Before I could get my long gun from the cabin, that bear had lit a shuck out of there. Rip let him go when he got out of our clearing, 'cause he weren't mad, just not in a mood to share."

Now Paw had taught me not to lie, but he also taught me that a yarn was just that, a yarn. It weren't really a lie, so I commenced to spin this one out.

"Another time, a feller tried to hit him with a hickory stick. Now that made him right angry and he commenced to chewin' that feller's arm near off. Lucky I was near enough to get him loose and get the man to the doctor. That arm will never be the same, but at least the doc was able to save it."

By now, that cowboy seemed to have lost his mad, and weren't looking near as mean as before. "Well, as long as he stays out of the way, I reckon he's alright."

"In fact, we was just leavin'." I called Rip to heel and we walked away, leaving a couple of more sober cowboys behind.

~ ~ ~ ~ ~

"Can you direct me to Captain Ford's room?" I asked the counterman at the hotel. I planned to waste no time talking with the Captain about a job.

"Upstairs, room 207."

Standing in front of that door, I thought of the step I was about to take. Was it the right thing for me? Regardless, I had to have money from somewhere before I could go back to the Nation, so I steeled myself and rapped on the door.

The man who opened the door wasn't what I expected. I reckon his reputation had me believin' he was seven feet tall and wide as a barn door. Instead, I saw a clean-shaven man a bit above average in height, with a touch of gray in his hair. He was well dressed, with a waistcoat and pressed trousers, sporting a ruffled front white shirt.

"Yes?" His eyebrows arched slightly as he took me in, lookin' me up and down.

"Sorry to disturb you, Captain," I said, "But I hear you're lookin' for men to ride west with you."

"And?" The eyebrows remained up.

"Well, Sir, if you ain't already found them, I'd be mighty pleased to accompany you. My name is Jonathon Stout."

He just stood in the doorway for a minute. "Forgive my rudeness." He stepped back, "Please come in and have a seat."

Takin' off my hat, I followed him into the room and looked around as he headed for a desk piled high with maps and papers. He took the seat behind the desk, and I sat in one of the two matching armchairs in front.

"So, you think you'd like to be a Ranger," he said with a small smile. "And you have come to be an Indian fighter, I suppose?"

As he spoke, he continued his appraisal of me. What he saw was a man of eighteen years, dressed in a homespun shirt and buckskin britches, standin' six foot and one inch tall and weighing about 195 pounds. I was glad I'd had my braids cut, as he again looked me over good. His gaze paused at the homemade holster holdin' my Walker Colt, then continued down to my moccasin-clad feet.

Other than that, I looked normal enough. There were plenty of men wearin' buckskin; I'd heard the captain himself wore them on the trail, and my hat was typical of these parts. I wore it with a flattened, creased crown, instead of rounded, but some men preferred it the other way. Either way, it worked fine as a basin to water my horse or hold shavin' water.

"I couldn't help but notice your footwear, do you own boots?"

"No Sir, but I can surely get me some."

"Well, it's more for protection of the leg than anything. We do some hard riding through chaparral and mesquite, not to mention the occasional cactus; boot are mighty handy."

I felt a glimmer of hope. He talked like he was considering hirin' me.

"Another thing that intrigues me is that holster, Mister Stout. Where did you come across it?"

"I made it myself, Captain." I proceeded to tell him about my time alone at the cabin after Paw was killed. He cocked his head to one side and gave a small nod, but he wasn't through yet. I'd heard he was a good judge of men, and I knew this was the judgin' part; I hoped it was good so far.

"Well, Mister Stout, that appears special made for a fast draw. Do you by chance consider yourself a gunman?"

"Not at all, Sir. I had little else to do back then, so I whiled away many an hour figurin' this out, and practicing. Not to be a gunman, but to be able to protect myself, if need be."

It was obvious the captain was an educated man, and was said to have a real head for strategy to go along with his courage.

"But, Sir, you can use it if you need to? Would you have a problem taking a life?"

"Captain, I have regrettably had to do so already. It is not something I speak of with pride, but it also does not weigh me down, as it was deserved in each case and was a matter of self-defense. There is evil in this land, and men must do what it takes to confront it."

"What do you think of Indians, who may not appear evil?"

"Sir, you should know that I was married to a Choctaw girl, and found her people to be among the best. She was stolen by some Shawnee braves and I later had to kill one of them when they attacked my camp. The second one, I let live. I never wish to harm innocent people, but dispensing justice to those who are not innocent is something I can do."

"Well said, Mister Stout. Pay is one dollar and a quarter per day, and found. You provide a good horse, a long gun, and a pistol. We try to provide food, ammunition, and provisions.

"When I say 'try', I mean just that. There are many times we must live off the land, and it is not always feasible to carry everything we need. We may, or may not, have wagons, but usually only pack animals. Oft times it will be only you and your horse."

"The life of a Ranger is not glamorous, as some would make it, but is very hard. We seldom get to bathe, have limited time for relationships, and live on the trail. Food may get scarce; we often dine on coffee and beans, and danger lies at every turn. That said, do you still wish to accompany me?"

Hat in hand, I stood tall in front of him, "More than ever, Sir, more than ever."

Chapter 10

WHILE WAITING AROUND for further word from the governor, we spent our time in the camp outside of town. A few of the men had money for hotels, but most did not. When I first arrived, I managed to meet Bud Cole; it was an unusual meeting.

As I rode in and dismounted from the roan, a tall, skinny galoot come amblin' over, lookin' like a crooked fence rail. Sandy hair poked out from under his hat and down the back to his collar. He looked me over, spat once, and said, "What we got here? Looks like half Comanche to me."

"Well, hell," I thought, "Gonna have to fight already." But, I looked him in the eye and said, "Nope. Half wildcat, and the other half is just mean."

He let out with a guffaw that would shame a jackass, and slapped me on the back. "Now I'm gonna like this feller, he shore ain't got no back up in him. Name's Bud Cole, Mister Wildcat, what's yore'n?"

No way could you stay mad at this funnin', so I answered, "Jonathon Stout, Mister Cole, at your service."

"Aw, hell, my paw was Mister Cole, I'm just Bud. Some folks calls me 'Beanpole', but I ain't never figured why."

"Folks call me Jon. And I sure enough don't know why anybody'd call you 'Beanpole', what with you bein' so fat and all."

This brought another guffaw, another slap on the back, and he became an instant friend. I reckoned he was quite a character, and he proved me right at every turn. There wasn't a mean bone in him, but his funnin' could get rude at times. No harm meant; it was just his way, always lookin' at the fun side of things.

A couple of days later, I decided to go get me a pair of them high top boots, and Bud rode along. On the way to town, he commenced to talkin', "Whereabouts you hail from Mister Wildcat?"

"Now Bud, you know my name, and unless you want me to call you 'Beanpole', you need to use it. To answer your question, I'm from the Kiamichi Mountains, but my maw and paw was from old Virginia."

"My maw died when I was born, and Paw moved me and him to the Indian Territories. He was killed when I was fifteen, and I been on my own ever since. How about you?"

"Well, I was born and reared in east Tennessee, but a gal run me off from there, so I decide to see what all the hoopla was about down here in Texas."

"A gal run you off? How'd that happen?" Right away, I regretted askin'.

"Well, it seems she done set her mind on marryin' up with me. The problem was, she was a big ol' gal, and ugly enough to make a hog run away from home. Why, she could out rassle near every man in the holler, includin' me.

"Her paw, now, he was downright mean. Dumb enough to stick his head in a sack full of rattlesnakes, just to see what the noise was, but mean as a mountain cat with a sore tail.

"Once she decided we was gittin' hitched, he fell right in with the ideer, and commenced to callin' me 'Son', and such like. I reckon he wanted to git her wed so's they'd have more groceries at home.

"Anyhow," he kept goin', "That gal chased me all over the hills. Every time I turned around, there she was, just a grinnin' and gigglin' at me. It begun to make me right nervous.

"Well Sir, I commenced to hidin' every time I seen her, but that didn't work. She was stubborn as a long-eared mule, and figured out all my good hideouts. She just wouldn't let up, and kept on cooin' and grinnin'.

"Now I begun to get somewhat skeered, on account of her paw had his own mind fixed on us ridin' double, and I figured he'd kill me grave-yard dead if I broke his little girl's heart.

"There's one good thing about bein' skeered; it'll keep you from getting' dead if you use it right. So, one night I come to the conclusion I was either gonna have to get hitched to that heifer, or make tracks outta' there. So, here I be."

After that long-winded speech, I just rode quiet while Bud caught his breath. I was afraid to say more, but that didn't stop Bud.

Lookin' off to the west, at some big black clouds building up out there, Bud asked me, "Say, did you ever see one of them twister storms?" He didn't wait for an answer.

"Why Pard, them things can be up to a mile wide and can go on for a hunnerd miles, just twistin' around and tearin' up jake. I heard tell of one that picked up a whole herd of cows in Texas, and didn't put 'em down 'til they was plumb up in the Nations. They was all alive when it set 'em down, but they couldn't walk straight for a month, and the milkers didn't give nothing but buttermilk for two whole weeks.

"The feller whose place they landed on allowed as how he was gonna keep 'em. He said the Lord done brought 'em, and the Lord would have to take 'em away."

Course that Texas feller heard about them, and tried to get 'em back. The court sided with the other feller, though, and agreed the Lord must of brung 'em. That was some mad Texan.

"Them's the dangdest things, tear a big ol' tree out by the roots, but never upset a baby's covers. I shore hope we get to see one."

There was one thing about Bud, you never knew if he was tellin' tales, or speaking true. Either way, he was sure entertaining.

When we got into town, Bud headed for the saloon to wet his whistle and I went on over to the boot shop. The old feller who ran the place had a few pairs of ready-mades, but nothin' in my size, so he measured me for a new pair. He said he'd have 'em ready in about a week, and would even stamp a star on each side and put my initials inside.

That sounded good to me, so I gave him my down payment and went to meet Bud. As soon as the saloon door closed behind me, the tension was obvious. Instead of the usual loud talk, tinkling chips, and slap of cards, it was quiet as a moonless night with a cougar on the prowl.

Bud was down toward the end of the bar, facing off with two big yahoos. Wearin' his usual grin, his hands at his sides, he was sayin', "Now fellers, ya'll know I was joshin', what for do you want to get mad? I meant no harm when I said ya'll was ugly as homemade dirt soup, and you gotta' admit ya'll ain't real purty.

"Now, come on and let me buy you both a drink and we'll just forget it. I'll even say I'm sorry ya'll are ugly, if you apologize for commentin' on my own slim attributes. My friends can do that, but I don't know you gents."

They took a step closer to Bud, and I used that as a chance to ease on down the bar toward the action. One of them said, "Why don't we just knock that silly grin off yore face instead."

Both men outweighed Bud by quite a bit, but then who don't? And, they was pretty ugly, so I saw his point, but we didn't need no trouble in town.

"Well," Bud drawled, "mostly 'cause that'd be hard on yore health, I reckon. Funnin' is one thing, but messin' with my purty smile ain't no fun."

All this time, I'd been easin' in closer, and saw the one nearest me make up his mind. As he doubled his fist and started to swing, I set my feet and hooked his arm just above the elbow. That brought a sudden stop to his swing, and he stumbled back a step or two, caught totally by surprise.

For a minute, he just stood there, wonderin' where I'd come from, I reckon. I told him, "Friend, I got no beef with you, and I reckon Bud can take care of hisself, but two agin one is just bad manners. Let's you and me sit this one out."

He must have mistook that for backin' down, 'cause he growled, "The hell you say," as he started to swing again—at me this time.

Now with all the hours me and Paw had spent practicing wrestlin', boxin', and Indian throws, I had no problem slippin' his roundhouse swing. A hard push in his back, as he turned, put him hard up against the bar. He caught his breath for a second, then he turned around to face me again.

Sneakin' a look at Bud, I saw his head and shoulders swaying like a coiled snake's head, side to side, back, then forward, before movin' just out of reach again. The man tryin' to hit him could never get a shot in, just kept missin'.

Bud hadn't laid a hand on him yet, but his grin was starting to fade. He slid away again, and said, "Now Mister, ya'll don't need to keep up with this ruckus, I might be forced to hurt you."

"Hold still, damn you, yore like fightin' smoke."

"How about you give it up now, yore about to get on my nerves." Bud gave him one more chance. The man took one more wild swing at Bud's head, missin' again, but this time Bud answered with the fastest uppercut I ever saw. The man's eyes bugged out, his knees buckled, and he hit the floor.

There wasn't time to see more, since my opponent had decided to take my head off about then. He only had one punch, a wild roundhouse that would do lots of damage if it landed. This time, I ducked under it and smacked him right smartly upside the head with a right hook. That slowed him down some.

He shook his head like a bull elk gettin' in the mood, looked around at his partner stretched out on the floor, and Bud leanin' on the bar, still grinnin'.

"I said I got no beef with you," I told him, "Are you ready for that beer now?"

He started to set up again, but then seemed to find some sense. Lookin real thoughtful, he asked, "Buy my friend one, too?"

"Why shore," Bud answered, "I'll buy ya'll a couple, if you want." He reached down and helped the other man to his feet, brushed him off, and said, "Set 'em up, Barkeep."

That's how we became acquainted with Jim and Lou Hanny, who was to become Rangers, and friends.

~ ~ ~ ~ ~

We finally got our orders, and left out from Austin town in February. Governor Runnels took office in January, made John Ford a Major, and gave him command of all Ranger forces. The state Congress passed the law they needed, and Major Ford headed us west.

We was strung out for a ways, having about a hundred men, two wagons, and an ambulance, plus pack animals. As we made our way westward, the weather began to warm, and bluebonnets and Indian paintbrushes covered whole hills in red and blue blossoms.

I also got to see some of the biggest horns I'd ever seen on cattle. It seems the man who told me about them long-horns wasn't just tellin' tall tales after all. Some of them was huge.

Further north and west, the land began to flatten out and prairie grass was everywhere. Mesquite was the predominant tree, and they growed in great bunches. The land here began to remind me of the Great Plains where I had searched so long for Mourning Dove and Little Fawn. It wasn't a pleasant memory.

By the time we got to Brown County, we had begun to see the effects of the depredations of Indians and bandits. Major Ford said it was obvious the reports had not been exaggerated, since we found many farms and small ranches deserted, empty of all but a few cattle left foraging.

Pillaged homes and burned out buildings were scattered about the landscape, with even small settlements left empty. The people had fled to areas of more population, abandoning their land and their dreams.

The Major made time to talk with all of his men every so often, and one night we had a confab, just me, him, and Bud.

"I've notified the Governor," he said, "and he has advised me to pursue the Indians as far as possible, and put an end to these raids. He also told me I could fire John Conner, a political appointee, and his so-called 'minute men'."

"Major," Bud asked, "how far do you plan to chase the Comanche, if we find 'em?"

"As far as necessary. Even into the Indian Territory if need be. Our job is to stop the raids into Texas, and with God's help, we will do so."

Later, the Major told us that some of John Conner's friends had raised cane with the governor, and Governor Runnels had sent him a letter saying, "If you need leaders, appoint them, but I will object to John Conner or one-eyed Indians as commanders." Seemed pretty plain to me, and we all got a good laugh from it.

By now, we were itchin' for some action. A force of friendly Indians, led by a Captain Ross, met up with us and we broke into four units, all sweepin' to the north. When some of the scouts reported that they had evidence of Comanche camps across the Red River, we rejoined forces at Cottonwood Springs, and headed up that way.

With a hundred and thirteen friendly Indians and over a hundred Rangers, we made a large force. The Major told us he was goin' to cross into Indian Territory, and we could stay in Texas, or come along. Bein' ready for a fight, and wanting to settle the issue, we all went.

Heading deeper into the Comanche's lands, we used all the stealth that a party that big could use. About the middle of May, scouts finally reported a hunting camp nearby. We attacked it the next morning, killing all but a couple of braves who got away and rode north as fast as their horses could carry them.

In pursuit, we topped a rise and saw a very big Comanche camp just across the Canadian River, on Cherokee land. Bein' forewarned, they was ready for us, some still scramblin' for their horses, but forming up to be a big force that Ford later said equaled at least 300.

About that time, the strangest thing I had yet seen went to paradin' across in front of those Comanche. Turns out, it was a chief called Iron Jacket. He had found some old Spanish armor, and wore it into battle, claiming it made him bul-letproof.

When he come prancin' out in front of them Indians, six or eight of our force decided to test his claim. Him and his horse both went down in a heap, shot several times. So much for bein' bulletproof, I reckon.

Crossin' the Canadian and wading into them Indians, we fired off our long guns first. Not taking time to reload, eve-rybody pulled out their pistols and commenced to enter the fray. Like most of the Rangers, I had bought another cylinder for my pistol, and kept it loaded. It took too much time to reload otherwise. Many carried two, or even three, loaded pistols in their belt.

While there was already some hand-to-hand fights, most of the Comanche scattered in all directions, with small groups of Rangers or our Indians right behind them. Me, Bud, and three others took out after a bunch headed west.

They'd ride hard, stop, turn, and fire, then spin and run some more. Mostly, they was armed with bows, but a Co-manche could do lots of damage with them. In this case, they only let us get within range of our pistols.

Our first volley emptied two horses and I saw another buck grab his arm, but manage to hold on. When we contin-ued to fire, another Comanche hit the dust and the rest threw down their weapons and pulled to a halt. They had taken all the damage they wanted. Dismounting, the fog of gunpowder making a stifling odor, I grabbed up any guns, leaving the bows, and we headed back with our prisoners.

By now the fight had spread out considerably, and people were scattered all over the place, mostly in small groups. Off to the left, I noticed a few Rangers in a skirmish that seemed to be goin' the wrong way. A couple of men were still mounted, firing into the band of Indians before them, but there was three on the ground, fighting with empty guns as clubs. Hollerin' at Bud, I spurred my mount that way, with him and Rip right behind.

I had swapped cylinders after the last tussle, so I had loads left. Ridin' the roan directly at one of the mounted warriors, I shot him point blank and he threw up his arms as he fell from his horse.

The roan slid to a stop at my tug on the reins and, not wanting to shoot at such close combat, I leaped from the saddle onto the back of one of the braves trying to get at Major Ford, who turned out to be in the fray, swingin' his gun by the barrel like a fence post, keepin' some distance between them, his pistol empty.

Taking that brave down, I saw Rip tear into another of them, and the Major swung again, crackin' one over the skull. In short order, we had got the best of them and I called Rip off. The mounted ones headed for the hills again, with Rangers hot on their tails.

Well, when it was all done, that fight had spread out for miles, and lasted over seven hours. Rangers and Indians come streaming back by the bunch, bringing back about 300 horses and eighteen prisoners. Major Ford said the dead numbered 76, with only two of our men killed and two wounded. By trying to best us in a running fight, the Comanche played into our strengths, revolving pistols with extra cylinders already loaded. That gave us a lot more firepower than they had.

Scouts reported that Buffalo Hump, another Comanche chief, was nearby with another large force but, with wore out horses and men, the Major decided we'd done enough schoolin' for one day. After this fight, the Comanche would likely steer clear of Texas for a while.

The next day, we headed back to Texas. I had some different feelin's about that fight. I knowed we had to do it if the country was to be safe for the settlers in west Texas, but somehow it didn't seem right. The Comanche was here before us, and they was just protectin' their way of life, so I felt bad for them. Still, I had sworn to do as the Rangers would have me do, so that part felt okay. It was plumb confusin' and I reckon I weren't cut out for takin' the fight to them. From now on, only if my life or somebody else's life was in danger would I fight. That decision made me feel better.

By the time we got back to Camp Runnels, named for the governor, we'd been gone from there a full month. The trail had been so hard that both wagons and the ambulance finally give out and had to be left behind. They was just too broke up to keep fixin'. All in all, it had been a hard trek.

Chapter 11

ALL THE TIME we'd been gone from Austin, my mind had never been far from Mourning Dove and her fate. I just couldn't accept that she was gone forever, and my rest was often interrupted by dreams of finding her. After our adventure across the Red, into the Indian Territories, I was even more thoughtful.

Paw had told me to be as good a man as I could be, and to follow my heart. Well, my heart was still up north with the Choctaw people and my bride, wherever she was. One day, ridin' along beside Bud, I commenced to talkin' about it. He knew some about my bein' bushwhacked, and how I come to be with the Choctaw, but I'd never shared all of the story with him. Now, I felt the need to let it all out; maybe it would help me to see it more clearly.

"Bud, you know about me bein' with the Choctaw for a while, but I never told you I was married to Owl Feather's granddaughter. She was tryin' to spoon some broth down me when I first come around after bein' shot, and I plumb fell in love right on the spot. She's pretty as a speckled pup, bright as a sunrise, and sweeter than bear honey. It took me a long time to heal, and we just hit it off."

Bud cut his eyes at me, but didn't say a word. Just waited for me to go on, knowin' I had something on my mind.

"After a lot of joshin' from her people, I finally learned how to court her, Choctaw style, and proceeded to do just that, Finally, we was married. I figured my life was complete and I'd have the family I dreamed of after losin' Paw like I did. But it wasn't meant to be, I reckon. Some Shawnee bucks, just young'uns lookin' for some mischief, caught her and her friend, Little Fawn, out pickin' berries one day while the men was all huntin'. They stole the girls away and me and Leaping Deer hunted all summer for them, with no luck."

Again, I felt Bud's eyes on me, but still no words from him. He seemed to tense up some when I told him of the girls capture, but said nothin'.

I rattled on, like a dam had busted inside me, and it all come gushin' out. "I finally found the camp of the bucks who took her, in the dead of winter, and I had to kill one of 'em when they snuck up on my camp in the midst of a blizzard. The second one told me they had sold the girls to some Cheyenne, for camp slaves, and they had gone far to the west and north with them."

The whole story come pourin' out of me, including the meeting with the Wiggins brothers in Fort Towson. Bud's eyebrows came up at the tellin' of that and he looked at me with either surprise or respect; I weren't sure.

"Bud, I just can't rest easy knowin' my bride is somewhere up there, maybe waitin' for me to come get her. I listened when Owl Feather told me it was hopeless, but my heart just won't be still. It bothers me somethin' awful at times."

"Well, when are we headin' north?" Bud asked after hearin' me out.

"Huh?" I stammered. "You think I should go?"

"Why, hell yeah," he said, "I knowed somethin' was stuck in yore craw but didn't know what. Now I do, so we gotta' go fix it, one way or another."

"You want to go along?" I asked before thinking it through.

"Boy, if you don't know me by now, you ain't near as bright as I give you credit for. For sure I'm goin'. I ain't never seen that country, and I always had a hankerin' to."

"Bud, you just convinced me. I know now that I'd never rest easy until I find out the truth of what happened to her. We'll tell the Major that we'll be leavin' when we get back to Austin. Our six month hitch is already up anyhow."

"Now yore talkin'," Bud said. "Yee-haw, another adventure!"

Sometimes I swear his brain was pea sized, but his heart was big as all outdoors.

The next day, we spurred up to ride with Major Ford, near the front of the troop. We rode in silence for a bit, then I spoke, "Major, I reckon me and Bud will be ridin' on as soon as we get mustered out in Austin. I've surely enjoyed ridin' with you and have learned a lot about the meaning of leadership, but I must return to the Indian Territories."

"Mister Stout," he replied, "I have ridden with, and fought with, many men. Few of them approach your caliber. I shall give you a letter of commendation and introduction upon our return, and you will always be welcome to ride with me should you come back this way."

"Thank you, Sir. Your comments are appreciated."

"You are a courageous man, Jon. Knowing you has been a pleasure, and I am sure you will go far in our bounteous country."

At these words we parted. He did have a letter delivered to me back in camp, and I tucked it away for safekeeping. We never spoke again, but I would always remember him as a brave, forthright, and honest man. I would later hear much of his exploits as a Texas Ranger.

~ ~ ~ ~ ~

When we got paid off in Austin town, me and Bud both felt rich. A dollar and a quarter a day don't sound like a lot, but getting' most of it in one pile will weigh a man down with cash.

The roan had been gettin' long in the tooth when Paw was killed, and the recent travels had showed me he needed to slow down some. I had talked with the Ranger quartermaster about one of the horses we had captured from the Comanche. He was a big, well-muscled buckskin the color of tanned hide with a black mane and tail, and I bought him as soon as we got paid. Bein' as I was in on the capture, I got a real good price on both him and a better saddle.

He was tall and had wide shoulders. A long neck carried his head proudly high, and a black forelock set off the tan color of his face. This horse, I decided to give a name to. 'Buck' seemed a good fit, 'cause of his tendency to be frisky in the mornin' and the color of his hide. So, Buck it was. The roan had pulled my travois and sometimes carried a pack, so I had no problem usin' him as a packhorse. It was a lot easier on him than carryin' me.

It was hades hot in Austin when we pulled shanks and headed north. The heat and humidity was enough to make a horned toad hunt a waterhole. This was my first time to enjoy a south Texas summer, and I weren't terribly impressed. Why, a man could bathe every week and still stink up a pig-sty within a couple of days. Since some of the Rangers in camp didn't bathe every week, or every month for that matter, it was a pleasure to leave there.

Travelin' with Bud was an experience in itself. I knew he'd fit right in with my Choctaw family, 'cause they loved a man who could laugh, and make them laugh with him. Once more I was bound for the Red River, but this time I was goin' home and my head was right.

Since I had told Bud about Sam Maxey, we stopped by Paris to see him on our way north, and to spend a day restin' up and gettin' a good feed. This time, I called Rip on in with us so Sam could meet him, too. When I made the introductions, Rip offered his paw, like a real gentleman, and I saw Sam was mighty impressed with him. He heaped lots of praise on him, which Rip just ate up. I told Sam how Rip had saved my life, at least twice, but made sure Rip didn't hear me. He'd get the big head if he knew how brave I thought he was, and it was big enough already.

Anyway, me and Bud spent the better part of the day jawin' with Sam and some other folks around town. Pretty soon, after a couple of beers, Bud got off on one of his tales and I figured he'd plumb embarrass us before he got done. But, Sam had a surprise for us both.

"Why, Bud," he says, "That reminds me of a terrible experience I had during the Mexican war. I'd gotten separated from my command, and was trying too sneak back to our lines. Problem was, I had to cross the Mexican line, surrounded by their army, and the area was full of dead, dry mesquite brush. I would be hard pressed to make it.

"Sure enough, just as I saw our campfires, that dry brush made too much noise and I heard a shout of 'Alto!' which is Mexican for Halt! I knew I was in deep trouble and hunkered down right there, hopin' they had only heard something, but not spotted me. But," he says, "they had, and soon forced me out of there at the point of their bayonets.

"Boys, I admit I have never been so scared in my life. They took me into camp and brought out this Mexican Colonel with sashes, braids, gold bands, and medals all over him. He could tell by my uniform I was an officer, and he proceeded to tell me what all I was gonna go through before they shot me. Well, I knew it was over. Here I was in the middle of the Mexican army with a madman who wanted to torture and then execute me. My command didn't even know I was alive, so I had no hopes there, either. Yep, I was done for."

Sam paused here to sip from his drink and stare thoughtfully at the wall. Time passed.

"Well, how the hell did you escape?" Bud could wait no longer.

"Oh, I just told that Colonel that I knew Bud Cole and Jonathon Stout, Texas Rangers, and he fell to his knees and begged me to go."

The whole group broke up laughin', including me, and Bud looked plumb flabbergasted for a minute. Then he cracked a big grin and said, "Damned if you ain't a ring-tailed Texan for shore. I'm right proud to know you, Mister Maxey."

After a jovial evening with the Texans, we got a room for the night and pulled out early the next day for Choctaw country.

Chapter 12

SITTIN' UP ON THE HILL overlookin' Pine Ridge, I could see
no changes since I'd left. We'd bypassed Fort Towson and
headed straight up here. I could see somebody movin'
around outside the store, but couldn't make 'em out. There
was smoke comin' from a couple of chimneys, including the
store's, and we could easily make out the big Missouri mules
in Dave Billings' stable yard. Rip must have recognized the
place, 'cause he had already gone ahead of us, lookin' for his
lady friend, I reckon.

We made our way down to the front of the store, still
with only the one sign, sayin' simply "Store" on it. Hitchin'
our animals to the rail, we stepped onto the porch and inside.
The same little bell tinkled out our arrival, and Sarge's head
appeared around the corner of the door leading back to their
livin' quarters. "Be right with you, I'm . . ." he started to say,
then stopped and stared for a minute.

Sarge rushed out front and wrung my hand, pumpin' it
like it was a broken pump handle, with him bein' mighty
thirsty. "Lawassa," he shouted to his wife, "Come see who's
done drug up in our store.

"By God, Boy, I never figured to see you again. How
you been? Did you go Rangerin'? What's been happenin'?"

"Whoa, Sarge." I laughed. "Slow down a mite. We'll get
to all that, but me and my pard, Bud, could use a shot to cut
the dust, and then some of yore world famous coffee. Top
that off with lots of Lawassa's home cookin', and you'll find
two happy hombres."

"Why Son, that'll be easy enough, set yourselves right
down there and let me go get the good bottle. This is worth
celebratin'."

At that moment, Lawassa's sweet face appeared from the
doorway. She was a heavy woman, but not overly so, with

dark skin and long black braids, shot with gray. I recollect Sarge sayin' one time that she was Chickasaw.

She enveloped me in a big bear hug. "Bless you Boy, for comin' back to us. This old man has worried hisself sick over you."

"Now, Wassa, just you never mind all that. These boys are hungry, and besides, I told you he wouldn't stay away. Not with Mourning Dove still missin'."

"Sarge, you got it right." I said. "It took me long enough to come to my senses, but I finally did. Lawassa, this here is my friend, Bud. He don't look like much, but keep an eye on him. He's a regular rip-snorter sometimes.

"Bud, I want you to meet the finest cook in the country, and as sweet as they come. Don't get no thoughts on stealin' her though. She keeps a mean shotgun behind that door, and Sarge is mighty protective."

With smiles all around, everybody met and shook hands. Sarge poured us men a small snort and we sat down to spin some yarns. Hadn't nothing changed in the store since I was last there. The rockin' chairs was out on the front porch, and we had to pull the little table away from the wall to make room for the three of us on the benches. Lawassa went to check on the groceries.

"So tell me, Jon, what's been happenin' with you these last months."

"Well Sarge, I did join up with the Texas Rangers, and rode with Major Rip Ford to fight the Comanche. Bud was my sidekick, and we had a couple of good battles before we mustered out. I spent about seven months with 'em all told."

"We done 'em some damage, and I reckon they'll think hard before they raid Texans again." Bud interjected.

"I can remember what it was like," Sarge said, runnin' a hand over his nearly bald head. "Holdin' on to yore hair with one hand, and yore gun with the other. Them devils took years off my life, just bein' near them. Uh, I heered some talk about them Wiggins boys gettin' killed over to Fort Towson, Jon. They say it was you what done 'em. How'd that come about?"

"They just pushed one time too many, Sarge. I was in a world of hurt over Mourning Dove, and I was in no frame of mind to take any more off of them. If I hadn't taken 'em down, they'd have killed me for sure that time. I shot the one, then the other one that we called "Ugly" rushed and missed me with his first shot. I didn't miss"

"Well son, don't let it bear on you none. The law laid a lot of stealin' and dry-gulchin' on them later. They was wanted over to Fort Smith, and was gonna die soon enough, by rope or gun." Sarge made me feel a bit better with that news.

Lawassa brought out a big platter of fried pork chops, collard greens, and boiled potatoes, along with a stack of her plump biscuits. This was all followed by sweet potato pie washed down with cool sweet milk and coffee. It all disappeared down our gullets pretty fast, and Bud sat back with a big grin.

"Ma'am, " he says, "That there was the best grub I reckon I ever had the pleasure of surroundin'. No wonder Sarge is protective. I'd fight a grizzly for you if'n I was him."

Lawassa kind of giggled and tried to hide her smile. "Go on with you, now. You don't need to be butterin' me up to eat here again."

"Maybe not," Bud returned. "But I want to make sure you know my name when the vittles are served next time."

Sarge wouldn't take a dime for the meal, and insisted on pourin' us all another short one. We sat around talkin' of the happenin's for a while before Sarge said, "Some Indian friends of our'n have been keepin' their ears open for any word of two Choctaw women with a band of Cheyenne. They ain't heard anything definite, but there was some talk of a bunch camped out about two hunnerd miles to the north. The rumor was that there might be a couple of young women with them."

I looked over at Bud and he kind of nodded just as Sarge continued, "It's just rumor, Jon, so don't get yore hopes up too much."

I knew that's where we'd be going, though. About that time, the bell over the door tinkled its warning again, and Sarge stood to see who had come in.

"Why howdy, Christina," he called. "I'll be right there. Boys, come meet Sandy Billings' niece, Christina. She moved in with Sandy and Dave after her mother got the consumption and died a few months ago. She's been here about three months now. Lovely girl."

We stood and removed our hats as she walked toward us. This girl was truly lovely. Standin' about five foot three or so, she had eyes the color of a cloudless west Texas sky, and her honey colored hair lay in waves around her shoulders.

"Howdy Ma'am," I said, and nodded to her.

Sarge cut in, "Tina, you remember us talkin' about Jon Stout? Well, this is him, and his Ranger buddy, Bud Cole. Boys, this is Christina Jewel, Sandy's niece."

"Oh, Jonathon Stout." She smiled. "I've heard so much about you from Uncle Dave and Aunt Sandy. It's a pleasure to finally meet you."

"The pleasure is all mine, Ma'am. Please, call me Jon."

Bud hadn't said a word yet, and I turned to find him just standin' there with his jaw open, frozen like a chunk of long, skinny ice. The only thing movin' was his big hands, and they was twistin' his hat up into a wad.

I poked him in the ribs. "Bud, say hello to Miss Jewel."

"Huh?" He looked surprised to see me, and stammered before findin' his voice. "H-h-how do, Miss Jewel." He finally spit it out, but still hadn't fully closed his trap.

"Oh, you both must call me Tina." She smiled sweetly, showing straight white teeth and a dimple in her left cheek. "I insist."

"Y-y-yes Ma'am, uh, Miss Tina, uh . . . " Bud had suddenly developed a speech problem, and I knowed what it was, havin' suffered the same fate myself. He'd been smacked right between the eyes with the axe handle of love. Me and Sarge shared a grin without either of them noticing. Sarge had seen it, too.

"So what can I get you today, Tina?"

"Oh, Aunt Sandy needs a couple of tins of those special beans she uses when she makes up her baked beans," Tina replied, castin' a sideways look at Bud. He was still rooted to the spot, twistin' on that hat 'til I wondered if it would survive the punishment.

"Why shore, Hon, got 'em right here." Sarge reached behind him to a shelf loaded with tinned goods. "I'll just put them on their bill."

"Thank you so much." Tina answered him before turning again to me and Bud. "I surely hope to see more of you both. I'd love to hear of your adventures and travels."

"Oh, I'm sure you'll be seein' us." I snuck a look at a stupefied Bud. "I'm real sure we'll be around."

"Why shore you will. We're gonna have us a wing-ding fiesta tonight, to welcome Jon and his slow witted pardner home. Tell Dave and Sandy, and ya'll spread the word for folks to bring a dish. Have Dave bring his fiddle, and I'll play the wash board. We'll have a bang up time and ya'll can dance in the street."

"I'll just do that, Mister Wesely, and we'll be sure to let everyone know. Sounds like fun."

I couldn't resist. "Well, ya'll can dance if we can get Bud's feet unstuck from the floor, and his mouth wired shut."

Finally realizin' what was said, Bud flushed as red as a ripe apple, and gave his hat another twist, but still couldn't find his tongue.

"Until tonight then." Tina sashayed out the door.

~ ~ ~ ~ ~

Word spread like wildfire, and that night turned into a real shindig. People came from miles around, bringin' food and musical instruments, if they had 'em. Before they were done, they had a regular band set up on the porch of the store.

A long table was set up down the side of the store, and it was piled with all kinds of food. Everybody had plenty to eat and I enjoyed watchin' 'em all dance and have a good time. I weren't interested in dancin', but Tina made me get out with her for at least one do-si-do, then Sandy had to have one too.

The whole bunch was havin' a great time. Well, all except for Bud. I noticed he didn't eat much, and he just stood on the edge of the porch, behind the band, watchin' Tina whirl to the music. Every time she was turned his way, I could see her lookin' at him, too.

Finally, I couldn't stand it no more. I jabbed Bud hard in the ribs, "You need to get on out there and ask Tina to dance. If you don't, you'll be standin' right here tomorrow mornin', just a wonderin' what happened."

"I'd shore admire to dance with her, Pard, but I just cain't seem to get up my nerve. I ain't never been skeered of no woman before, but there's just somethin' about her."

"Bud, it's 'cause you really like her." I told him. "Now just get on out there and ask her."

He was again clutchin' his poor bedeviled hat and couldn't take his eyes off of Tina as he stumbled toward the street.

"Bud!" I cried out—too late. He missed the edge of the porch and stepped right off without even lookin' down. Bud sprawled head first into the street, causin' a great puff of dust to rise around him. He lay right at the edge of the dancers, who had all stopped when the band suddenly quit playin'.

Of course, everybody was lookin' at Bud, all sprawled out in the dirt, and he just laid there for a minute, catchin' his breath. Nobody wanted to laugh, afraid he might be hurt, but everybody seemed frozen in place.

Finally, Tina ran over to him and, putting a hand on his back asked, "Bud, are you okay?"

He rolled over, grinned up at her and said, "Yes Ma'am, I am now."

Somebody snickered, and then everybody just broke up. It was partly relief that he was all right, and partly the sight of him still sprawling in the dirt, hat still in his hand. He got up, brushed himself off with that poor lookin' hat, and smiled at Tina, "Now that I've entertained everybody, how about a dance?"

"Oh Bud! I thought you'd never ask." They turned to the band, Bud said, "Strike 'em up, boys," and they danced away, with people slappin' Bud on the back and smilin' to beat all.

"That Bud makes quite an entrance, don't he?" I looked around to find Sarge standin' at my side.

"That he does, Sarge, that he does."

"I reckon ya'll will be leavin' out soon," he said, "and I wanted to talk to you some before you go."

"Sure thing, why don't we step into the store for a few minutes. I don't think we'll be missed."

We went on back through the store and into the house part. Sarge wiped out a couple of glasses and poured us a short drink as we sat down at the table.

"Son, I'm real concerned about ya'll goin' into the plains again. You know there ain't no law up there 'cept a few U S Marshals outta' Fort Smith. That country is fillin' up with bandits and outlaws, and the Indians ain't liking what's goin' on, either. It's more dangerous now than before."

"That's what we've been hearin', Sarge, and we know we'll have to ride alert every minute, but I have to go."

"I reckon I knew that, Jon, but I still worry, and Lawassa does too, even if she don't say it."

"I know, and ya'll are about the best friends a man could have. We're goin' to stop by and spend a day or so with Owl Feather, and I figure Leaping Deer will want to go along, too. That'll make three of us, and ain't none of us tenderfeet. Leastways, not any more."

"Well," he continued, "I just wanted you to be aware of how things is, and know to be extra careful. We pray that you find Mourning Dove this time, and that you finally get a chance to be happy.

"This country's growin' up fast, and it's having growin' pains. There's many good men and women out here, but there's many a bad one, too. They prey on the weak or the unprepared, and will kill to get what they want. Ya'll always keep that in mind."

"I plan to, Sarge, and I know Bud and Leaping Deer are as smart as they come, trail-wise. You and Lawassa just keep the coffee hot, we'll be back."

After a bit, Sarge allowed as how we should get back to the fun, so we went back outside. The band was windin' down, food had almost disappeared, and most folks was tuckin' their young ones into the back of wagons and buggies.

The last tune was a slow one, and only one other couple joined Bud and Tina in dancin' to it. Them two was movin' real slow and lookin' at each other with puppy dog eyes. Tina looked like a pixie doll in Buck's arms; she was so tiny next to his tall frame. It's a wonder she didn't get a neck ache from lookin' up at him so much. Of course, he had her laughin' most of the time. I'd heard women like a man who can make them laugh. If that was true, she'd sure enough like Bud.

When the song ended, Bud stood rooted to the spot, again, like he didn't know how to move. Tina finally reached up, pulled his head down, and kissed him on the cheek, "I had a real good time, Bud. I hope we can do it again sometime."

"Uh, yes Ma'am . . . Miss Tina, I mean, me too." He was back to bein' tongue-tied.

Givin' him a smile that could light up Texas, she headed for Dave and Sandy's house, leavin' him flat footed.

The very next mornin', me and Bud fixed the pack to the roan, saddled up, and said goodbye to Sarge and Lawassa. Bud kept lookin' down toward Dave's place, obviously looking for Tina, and she finally came out and headed our way.

"Surely you weren't leaving without a goodbye," she said, "I'd never have forgiven you."

"No Ma'am," Bud blushed red, "we was gonna ride down there if you didn't show up."

"Well, you had better. Here," she handed Bud a package wrapped in brown paper, "here's some muffins I made this morning, just for you. And Jon, of course."

"Why, thank you kindly, Tina. I'm shore they'll be mighty tasty." Bud replied.

"You two be extra careful, now. And Jon, I hope you find your bride."

"Thanks, Tina, I plan to stay as long as I need to this time. I have to know what happened to her, or it'll always eat at me. I'll find out somethin', even if I have to go clear to Canada."

"Well, good luck, and take care of my man for me." She smiled sweetly at Bud, flipped the hair off of her shoulder, and headed back toward the house.

I took the package of muffins away from Bud before he destroyed them the way he had done his hat, and mounted Buck, waitin' for Bud to mount up. I tell you what, if something didn't give soon, Bud was gonna get lock jaw with his mouth hangin' open. "Mount up, Pardner, and let's ride," I called.

Still starin' towards Tina, he missed the stirrup, and nearly fell into the dirt again. "Bud, you're gonna hurt yourself if you don't get a brain. That gal is more dangerous to you than a tribe of Comanche."

He mounted, givin' me a weak grin, "Did you hear her, Jon? She said, 'Her man'. Did you hear her?"

"Yeah, Bud, I heard her tell me to take care of you. The way you stumble, trip, and fall around her, she probably figures you're feeble minded or somethin'."

"I don't care. She called me 'her man'. Now ain't that somethin'?"

Sarge took each of our hands and shook 'em, givin' me a long look. "Remember what I said, Boy. Be careful out there."

"We will, Sarge." I spurred Buck gently, and we rode away. Lookin' back, we saw Sarge on the porch and Tina standin' in the street in front of the livery. Neither waved, but just looked kinda lost.

~ ~ ~ ~ ~

A couple of good days had us close to the Choctaw camp where Owl Feather lived, and where I had wed Mourning Dove. It was getting' late when we rode in, me lookin' around for any changes. Our cabin still stood near to Owl Feather's, and it was still empty. We found him sittin' on a bench outside his door.

"Welcome home, my son." He spoke in Choctaw.

Answering in the same way, I said, "Thank you, Grandfather. How are you this day?"

"The days are long and hard with my family gone from me, but I feel it will get better soon. Who is your friend?"

"Grandfather, this is Bud Cole. He is a great friend, and rode at my side for many miles. He has come to aid me in my quest."

"That is good. Why have you decided to return to the hunt?"

"My heart was empty. I could not fill it with time; I could only ease it a little. I must find my wife, your granddaughter, to fill it again."

"Yes, after you left I understood that I had told you wrong. I should have said to look forever, but I thought it was true, what I said to you."

"It is not your fault, Grandfather, but mine. I was too unsure of my ability to find her, so I took the wrong road. Now, I know the path I must follow. It is good to be home."

"It is always good to go home. Come, you and your friend. Hannah Whitehorse has brought me some venison. We eat now." He led us into his cabin, stoppin' to scratch Rip around the ears and ask, "And how is the devil wolf this day?" Rip grinned at him and licked his hand, then laid down beside the door.

Pretty soon, word of our arrival had spread and John Leaping Deer showed up at the door. "Waugh!" He cried. "Spirit Warrior has returned to us."

This caused Bud to cut me a funny look, a question in his eyes.

"Later, Bud." I said before greeting Leaping Deer. "How are you, my brother? Any papooses in your lodge yet?"

He laughed, "Of course. I waste no time making my family. Are we going back to the north?"

"Yes, Brother, we are. This is my friend, Bud Cole. He is riding with us. Are you sure you wish to leave your family, though?"

He nodded at Bud, who returned it. "I never wish to leave them, but some things a man must do. When do we leave?"

"Let us have this night to sit by the campfire with Owl Feather, eat, and tell stories of our travels. Bring your family and join us, and then we will leave tomorrow."

"It is done, Brother. We will return shortly." Then he was gone.

"Spirit Warrior?" Bud looked befuddled.

"It's a long story, Bud. I'm sure Leaping Deer will tell it sometime soon, he finds it funny."

So, that night we sat around the campfire and talked of things past and present. At one time or another, everybody in the camp came by to say hello and sit a spell. Bud really enjoyed the fun and laughter we all shared, and allowed as how he liked this family of mine.

Right about sunrise, Leaping Deer was waiting for us when we rolled up our sleeping gear and got ready to saddle up. He'd brought a sack of jerky and a haunch of smoked venison to add to the pack. We'd eat the venison in a couple of days, and then have jerky to chew on if we found no game, or didn't take time to hunt.

Once the pack was loaded and the horses saddled, we sat down to finish off the coffee before leavin'. Me and Bud had already ate a couple of sourdough biscuits and shared a tin of peaches.

"We have heard the talk you spoke of last night." Leaping Deer said. "There is supposed to be a band of Cheyenne camped on the Great Plains hunting buffalo about a week's ride from here. Maybe we should try there first."

"I reckon that's the plan," I answered. "It seems like the place to start. At the least, maybe we can get some information. I'm afraid the Cheyenne will be leavin' again for their winter homes if we don't hurry."

"Both girls were like my little sisters. I, like you, don't rest easy without knowing." He finished his coffee and kicked dirt over the fire that was still smoldering. "Let us ride. Waugh, the Spirit Warrior rides again, hide the children!" He laughed loudly as he rode away, leavin' Bud starin' after him.

Bud would find out the truth soon enough. I had retrieved my white buckskin suit, with the beaded front, from the cabin we'd built for Mourning Dove and me. Once we encountered an Indian camp, I'd put it on and share the story, unless Leaping Deer told it first.

Chapter 13

WITHIN A COUPLE OF DAYS, headed due north, the land had started to flatten out. I had talked with many of the men who rode with the Rangers, and some of them had come through the Great Plains on their way to Texas.

They spoke of a new fort, named for General Bennett Riley that had been built along the Oregon Trail to help protect travelers through that area. I figured we'd follow the Arkansas River north by west and then break off to head due north to the fort, if we had not run across the camp by then.

This would likely be the only place we could replenish our grub, ammunition, and such. This whole territory was pretty much uncharted, and I'd heard of no other towns or settlements near where we were goin'.

"What do ya' think, Jon? Any real chance we'll find 'em any time soon?"

"I doubt it, Bud. We'll just have to take what comes and hit every camp we come to. They're out there somewhere, and this time I'm gonna find 'em, come hell or high water."

The first camps we encountered was either Choctaw or Cherokee. They couldn't tell us any more than we already knew, so we kept on the trail.

Finally, Leaping Deer, who had been scouting out in front of us, came riding back sayin' he had found a Creek hunting camp ahead. It was time for the Spirit Warrior to put in an appearance. While I pulled the white buckskins out of my pack and got dressed, Leaping Deer told Bud the story of the Spirit Warrior and his devil wolf, accompanied by much laughter.

Bud gave me an evil grin, "Just wait 'til folks hear about this." He laughed out loud at the idea.

"No Sir," I said, "nobody knows outside of a very few. If the story got around, it would make my life a misery, and ruin the effect on the Indians we need to impress. This one stays under our hats."

"Aw shucks. I shore wanted to tell that one, it's a great story and would shore liven up a campfire."

"I know, Bud, but you gotta' keep this to yourself, okay?"

"Shore thing, Jon. I can keep a secret." That earned him a quick look from me, eyebrows raised.

"Well, I can if'n I want to."

I grinned at him and nodded. That much was true—if he wanted to. I reckon I could trust him on this.

All decked out, with Buck's mane and tail braided along with my grown out hair, it was decided that me and Leaping Deer would ride in together this time. Bud would stay with the packhorse and start settin' up camp. Rip would go with me and Leaping Deer only far enough to be seen, then he'd circle the camp waitin' for us to ride out.

The Creek was neighbors to the Choctaw and Cherokee, so we had no problem talkin' with them. Just the sight of Rip circlin' the camp, givin' them just brief glimpses of him, and me in my whites sittin' tall on the buckskin, had 'em in a friendly frame of mind. Besides, the Creek was mostly friendly anyways, at least for now. And this was a huntin' camp, not a war party, so they had their families with them.

After greeting a couple of the braves who rode out to meet us, we was escorted into camp. Once there, it was easy to see who was in charge. A tall, finely dressed brave stood alone in the center of camp, just lookin' at us approach. He wore two eagle feathers in his hair and his buckskin shirt was finely beaded in some intricate design. It was more than a match for mine, only it weren't white.

"Ya-ta-hay." I greeted him in the language of the plains, then switched to Choctaw, "My brother and I wish to speak with you. We come as friends."

Lookin' us both over real good, he asked, "How is it you speak the tongue so well?"

"My bride is of the Choctaw people, I learn from her and my brothers there. She is why we have come."

"Does the great yellow wolf travel with you?"

"He travels where he wishes. He just wishes to travel at my side most times."

Slowly nodding his head, he said, "Come, sit by my fire and we will smoke." I reckon the idea of a yeller wolf travelin' with a man such as I was all he needed to know about me.

We dismounted and sat on our haunches while he had a squaw fetch his pipe and tobacco. Nobody spoke until he had it packed and lit, and then offered the smoke to the four corners of the earth before takin' a puff. He passed it to me and I also offered up the smoke, then I passed it on to Leaping Deer.

"We have heard great stories of the Spirit Warrior and his demon wolf who fight together and can appear wherever they wish. Are you this warrior?" He broke the silence.

"I cannot say, my friend. I too have heard the stories but do not wish to frighten women and children by saying it is so."

"Huh," he grunted. "Why have you come here?"

"My wife was stolen two summers ago. I still seek word of her so that my lodge may again be full, and my spirit happy. It is said that she and a friend may be with a tribe nearby. I wish to know if you have heard this."

He sat on the ground, knees up, with his elbows resting on them as he contemplated the grass between his moccasined feet. After a moment, he looked up at me, "Yes, I have heard of this. A band of Cheyenne is said to have two women slaves with them in their camp. It is said they are young, and the braves seek them as wives. I know not where this camp is, only that it is in that direction." He pointed north.

"We thank you, my friend. My search may be shortened with your help. Now we must go, for the trail is long and my wife awaits me."

"I have heard of you, as I told you, and it is said that you are a good man whose quest is just. You chose to let one man live when you had his life in your hands. This tells me you are not evil. That is why I help you. May the Great Spirit ride with you, and know that you are welcome in my camp."

With that, I saluted him and we rode out of the camp. We knew more now than before, and my heart was poundin' in my chest. We may be closer than ever before to findin' the girls, and it sounded like they were still together.

Bud had the camp all set up and coffee boilin' in the pot when we got back. He had staked the horses out to graze, so we did the same with ours and proceeded to tell him of what we'd learned.

It was after dark by the time we ate and rolled out our bedrolls, so we settled in for an early night, and an early start tomorrow. I laid there thinkin' of Mourning Dove and our brief time together. Us bein' together was meant to be, and I'd not give up this time.

Night sounds on the plains was different from the woods. There was still the familiar dove and Bob White, but no sound of squirrels or frogs, unless you were near water. We had camped a ways back from the river, so I heard none.

I felt Rip easin' alongside me and stickin' his head under my hand. It was unusual for him to want to be so close, but I enjoyed it as I scratched his ears for him. He give out with a deep sigh, and drifted off. I figured I'd be awake all night, thinkin' of Mourning Dove, but I soon joined him in sleep.

I was up long before sun up, stirrin' up the fire and puttin' coffee on. When I put the skillet on the coals and started slicin' sowbelly into it, Bud stuck his head up.

"Dang Boy, you shore are in a hurry this mornin'"

"Yep, we got a far piece to travel, and I want to get in all the miles we can. Breakfast will be ready soon and coffee is ready now. Roll on out when you want some, I ain't bringin' you coffee in bed."

"Aww," he says, "You break my pore heart." He looked over at Leaping Deer's bedroll, ready to say somethin' smart, but found it empty.

"He's been gone about an hour," I told Bud, "scoutin' ahead. He'll be back soon to eat."

"Damn, I never even heard him stirrin'. He can be awful quiet, cain't he?"

"When he wants to be." I responded. "Bacon is ready, come on if you're gonna eat."

He sat up and tugged on his boots. We slept in everything but our hats and boots, or moccasins, so we'd be ready to go at a minute's notice if need be. It didn't do much for our clothes or our smell, but it was sure safer that way. We all slept with a gun at hand, too.

"Well, Pard, reckon we might be getting' close, huh?"

"I sure hope so, Bud. My hide feels like fleas are eatin' me one bite at a time. I need to find that girl."

"You shore it ain't fleas?" He asked. "What with that hound sleepin' with you and all?" Bud cracked one of his ready grins at me.

"You know, it might be fleas at that. I'll find a hole to bathe in today."

At the sound of a horse coming, we both looked up to see Leaping Deer ride in. He jumped from his horse and grabbed a cup, pourin' himself some coffee before he spoke.

"Nothing ahead that I find," he said. "Long ride to next camp I think."

"Well, it would be too easy if we found them in only a few days, I reckon. It must be another three or four days to Fort Riley, so we'll leave the river after tomorrow. Meanwhile, we'll stop wherever there's a camp, okay?"

"Sounds right to me," he announced. "If Bud don't take all day to get ready."

"Now look here," Bud sputtered, "I got to have my beauty sleep. There's a purty gal just pinin' away for me back in Pine Ridge, and she won't want me all wore out."

We all laughed at that, finished up our breakfast, such as it was, and got started on another long day. By late evenin' we'd only seen one camp along the river. It was a band of Cherokee, fishin' and smokin' their catch. I'd heard some of the plains tribes wouldn't eat fish, thinkin' it was dirty, but for others it was a staple of their diet. You just never knew about Indians.

After another night along the river, we headed due north the next day, towards Fort Riley. Along about noon, we come up on a couple in a wagon pulled by two big oxen. They looked downtrodden, what with the woman weepin' into her scarf, and the man settin' up on the seat with his face hard as rock.

He wore bib front overalls with straps on 'em and had his gray homespun shirt tucked in. On his head was a floppy old black hat like I used to wear. She was wearin' a long, green gingham dress and bonnet. Two kids had their heads stuck out the back of the wagon, a boy about twelve and a girl of ten or so. The little girl was cryin', too. Since the man was holdin' a shotgun in his hands, we kept ours in plain sight as we rode close enough to talk.

"What's the matter, Mister?" I asked him, never takin' my eyes off that shotgun. "Ya'll lost?"

He took a minute to stare at Leaping Deer and Bud, sittin' a few feet behind me, before answerin'. "I reckon we are," he said, "we was lookin' for Fort Riley, where we was to meet up with some other folks goin' west."

"Well Sir, that's where we're headed. It would be fine if ya'll went along with us. You're south of the trail."

"We might as well turn back!" cried the woman, "Them other fellers stole all our money, and a lot of our food. We can't go on."

"When did this happen?" I asked.

"'Bout an hour ago," the man answered. "We just now got things put back right, and didn't know which way to go from here."

Leaping Deer had been scoutin' around after hearin' the woman's words, and he gave me a nod, lookin' off to the west. "Four men," he said.

"How'd you know that?" The man wanted to know.

"He reads sign real good," I told him. "It's plain enough here in the grass."

Well, we had us what you'd call a problem, I reckon. Do we just leave these folks to their fate, or do we try and help them out? We didn't have no set schedule, but I sure wanted to keep on the trail while it was hot.

The man climbed down from his wagon and stood beside the front wheel while he talked, "We shore don't know what to do, gents. Those four rode in real peaceable lookin' and said 'Howdy.' When they found out we was alone, one of 'em pulled out his pistol and said, 'That's real bad news, folks. For ya'll, anyways.'

"He got us all out here by the wagon and a couple of 'em went inside and started throwin' our things out, lookin' through our stuff. The one with the pistol told me he'd beat me and the wife 'til I give him any cash money we had, or I could just hand it over. I believed him, so I give it to him."

"What did these gents look like?" I asked him.

"Well, the one with the gun was maybe twenty or so, short and stocky, with reddish colored hair. I heerd one of 'em call him 'Red'. He rode a grulla, and had him a good lookin' saddle, must of cost him a lot. The two who tore up our wagon was older, and wore run down boots and round brim hats. They all had six shooters 'cept one, who only had him a Bowie knife on his hip. He was a young'un, and he didn't get off his horse or say nothin' the whole time. Looked like he wanted to be somewheres else."

"They didn't take yore scattergun?" Bud asked.

"It was down under the seat. I didn't have a chance to git it out before we was covered, so they never found it."

I signaled Bud and Leaping Deer, and we rode a little piece away from the wagon. "What do ya'll think, boys? They got an hour head start, but might not be in no hurry, figurin' it'd be a long while before these folks got to any help."

Leaping Deer just looked over at them folks and nodded at me. Bud said, "Hell, Jon, we're Rangers ain't we? At least ex-Rangers, so we cain't just let this go."

"That's what I was thinkin', Bud, and Leaping Deer is on the same page as us. Let's go get their money back."

We rode back to the wagon and told them folks which way to head. "Just keep pointed at that rise yonder, and after you cross it, find another mark to head for. We'll catch up by tonight. Find a good place to camp but don't light no fire; we'll find you but you don't want nobody else to."

The man took off his hat. "I'm sorry Mister," he said, "I'm Ralph Long, and this here is my missus, Matilda. I plumb forgot my manners before."

"That's okay, Ralph. My name is Jonathon Stout, and these are my friends, Bud Cole and John Leaping Deer . . . he's Choctaw. We're gonna see if we can find those men and get your money back. Ya'll just head for the fort, like I said."

"I don't know how to ever repay you, Mister Stout. We'd be forever beholden."

"Well, we ain't got it yet, so save the thanks 'til we have. See you later."

I had Rip stay with these folks, and look after them. We'd be riding hard and I knew he'd be better off with them. We kicked up our horses and commenced to follow the trail west. The trail the men had left wasn't hard to follow. The grass was pretty tall and dry enough to leave a clear trail. We rode easy for a while, knowin' they was a ways ahead of us. I'd tied Horse to the wagon's tailgate, so we didn't have to drag him along with the packs.

After a while, we came upon some horse droppin's and Leaping Deer checked 'em out. "Still warm," he told me, "Not too far ahead now."

They was mostly walkin' their horses, but the sign showed them kickin' up to a trot now and then. We'd kept to an easy, ground eating lope that weren't hard on the horses or us, but it made good time. At the news they was close, me and Bud both pulled out our long guns, and Leaping Deer did the same when he remounted. We didn't plan to get caught off guard.

Another hour or so had us toppin' a small knoll to see four riders ahead. They was a ways off, but we kept on at our steady pace and started overtakin' them. Here in the plains, a man could see for miles if he had somethin' above ground level to look at. Four men on horses tended to stand out.

"They not see us yet," Leaping Deer said.

"Nope," I replied, "Looks like they ain't got a care. They ain't checkin' their back trail, that's for sure."

I knew they'd eventually turn and spot us, or hear us comin', but we was in range before they did. One of 'em turned and looked over his shoulder, and said somethin' to the others real quick. They all stopped pretty quick and turned to look at us.

We didn't raise our guns or nothin', just held 'em across our saddles and kept comin'. I shifted the long gun to my left hand and eased the hammer strap off my Colt. I saw Bud do the same, but we was far enough away that they didn't see it. The four of them waited for us. After all, they had us out-gunned so they thought they had nothin' to fear.

"Howdy fellers," said the stocky young one, "Ya'll appear to be ridin' the same way we are, want to ride together?"

Since both my friends looked at me, I reckon I was elected spokesman. "We would, Mister, but we have to be gettin' back to some folks we left behind us in a wagon. Seems they lost some money and we thought ya'll might have found it."

He grinned and dropped his right hand down to his thigh, next to where he had what appeared to be a .31 caliber Navy Colt ridin' in a tied down holster. The grips looked well worn, so I knew it had seen some use, but whether he had used it, or others before him, I had no way of knowin'.

"No Sir. I don't recollect findin' no money. Did you boys find any money?" He looked around at his friends, still wearin' that grin. They had stiffened when I first mentioned the folks in the wagon, but now they relaxed.

"Naw, Red, I ain't found no money. How about you, Jim?" The one who spoke looked to be thirty or so and wore a dirty brown shirt covered by a greasy vest. His pistol was pulled to the front of his belt, and half covered by his ample belly.

Jim, the other older one, chewed his cud for a minute, spat tobacco in the dirt at Buck's hooves, and sneered,

"Nope, but if'n I had I don't reckon I'd give it to no piss-ant kid like you."

I noticed the youngest one, maybe in his mid teens, easin' his horse back a little at a time. Since he carried no pistol, and his long gun was in the scabbard, I all but dismissed him. Besides, he looked plumb scared.

"Seems we got us a problem then, fellers. Them folks described you real good, and even told us yore names." I stretched that just a mite. "I reckon we're gonna have to ask you to step down so we can search you and your saddle-bags."

"The hell, you say!" Red made a grab for his belted Colt, but mine come out way faster. Just as he started to lift it, I shot him dead center and he flopped backwards off his horse.

I immediately turned my gun on Jim, who had his own out and raised toward Bud, and I pulled the trigger again. About the time I fired, I saw a red hole blossom on the right side of his rib cage, and then saw another one just below his heart as my bullet found it's mark. Me and Bud had shot at almost the same instant.

The one in the dirty vest had taken a bullet from Leaping Deer before he could get his iron clear of his belly. In a heartbeat, and a cloud of smoke, it was over.

I was real pleased that Buck had not moved a muscle, even with all the flame, noise, and smoke comin' from the guns around him. He wasn't the least bit skittish, and that made him even more valuable. A rock solid horse is a real find.

The kid with the knife had not even twitched. I looked at him and he raised his hands up beside his ears and stammered, "I . . . I got none of those folks money, Mister . . . honest. I don't like what they been doin', but didn't know how to get away from them without gettin' shot myself."

I opened my Colt and began reloadin'. "I believe you, Kid. You can ride on if you've a mind to, or you can go back with us. We're headin' to Fort Riley as soon as we get those folks money back to 'em—and you can put your hands down."

"Gee, thanks Mister. I'd be real pleased to ride back with you. I'd like to say I'm sorry to them wagon folks, too."

"Good enough for me, Kid. What do we call you?"

"Sam, Sir, Sam Ervin. My folks had a place down towards Texas, but the Comanche got my paw, and Maw died last year. I couldn't stay on by myself, so I just saddled up and headed somewheres there might be people, and I could get work. I met up with them fellers about a week ago. They seemed okay, 'til they robbed them folks."

His predicament reminded me of my own situation a few short years ago. We'd take him with us 'til he got somewhere safe, I reckoned.

Meantime, Bud and Leaping Deer had got down and was goin' through them bandits' pockets and saddlebags, after checkin' for any signs of life. They was all as dead as they'd ever be. None of us had missed.

Bud come up from beside Red's body with a sack of coins and a roll of paper money. He also pulled a sheet of paper out of Red's shirt pocket and unfolded it, handin' it up to me. It was a reward poster offerin' 500 dollars for Dolph Sims, also called "Red". The description fit him good, right down to his fancy saddle. He was wanted for robbery and murder.

"Sam, looks like you got in with some real bad men here. Probably lucky for you we came along. The law would likely have hung you all if you was caught ridin' with 'em."

"Land sakes! I never would'a even talked to 'em if I'd knowed that."

"Well, Kid, me and Bud was Texas Rangers, and Leaping Deer is as good as they come, so you're safe with us. My name is Jon, by the way, Jonathon Stout."

After we'd emptied their pockets and taken their weapons, Bud asked me, "Gonna bury 'em, Jon?"

"Nope, not unless you want to. I don't usually bury snakes, and I sure ain't readin' no words over them fellers. I say we ride before it gets any later. Bein' coyote food is all they deserve, in my book."

"Kinda the way I feel. I'm ready when you are."

The kid's horse was gettin' long in the tooth, and was swaybacked as a hammock. I told him to get on the grulla, and I'd write him out a paper on how he got it when we got to Fort Riley. I'd have the Commander or somebody witness it for him, just in case Red had stole it somewhere. He hesitated at first, but finally agreed so he wouldn't slow us up. We gathered the other horses and headed back.

There was some mighty happy faces around the wagon when we rode in and Bud dropped that sack in Mister Long's hands. After countin' up all the money, they got back every dime of theirs, and left us with over a hundred and eighty to split. I made Sam take a share, too, even though he protested.

He'd been right sorrowful on the way back, and nearly cried when he told them folks how sorry he was, and explained to them how he came to be with the outlaws. They understood, and now he was playin' games with the boy and girl while their folks held on to each other and smiled.

"Jon, you men renewed my faith in the human race," Mister Long kept sayin'. "Not many would have done what ya'll did, and asked for nothin' in return."

"There are more good people than bad," I responded, "But the bad ones make it rough on the good folks sometimes. We have to take 'em on when we can. I'm just proud we was able to help."

I think we all felt good on this day.

Chapter 14

WHAT WITH HAVIN' to ride at the oxen's pace, it taken us three more days to get to Fort Riley, instead of two. As we got closer to the fort, we began to see cabins and farms here and there. Folks tended to settle near the protection offered by the army, wherever it was found.

We said goodbye to the Long's and wished 'em luck on their journey, then I headed to the fort headquarters with Sam in tow. It was a pretty impressive buildin', bein' as how the fort was so new. The whole thing was impressive.

Two story buildings, made of native limestone, was scattered around an open parade ground. I counted twelve of these long buildings, which was for barracks and officers' quarters. A lot of soldiers was stationed here, for sure.

I broke out the letter that Major Ford had written for me and presented it to the sergeant sittin' behind a big wooden desk in the entry foyer, then I asked to see someone in charge. He looked me over good and took the letter from me kinda gingerly, with just his thumb and one finger. I reckon I weren't very impressive lookin', after so much time sleepin' in my clothes and all, but his attitude seemed to change as he read the letter.

"Please have a seat, Mister Stout." He pointed at some armchairs along the wall to my right. "I'll see who is available to meet with you."

Me and Sam set ourselves down in a couple of them chairs and looked around at the pictures on the walls. There was pictures of men in fancy uniforms with lots of gold braid, horses on the parade field, and some mighty fine lookin' gents in top hats and such. It was something to see, all right.

Pretty soon, the sergeant came back and said, "The Captain will see you, gentlemen. Right this way." He led us into a room somewhat smaller than the front room, but still good sized.

The Captain, I reckon it was, came out from behind his desk, a shade bigger than the sergeant's, and shook our hands. He handed my letter back to me. "Quite an endorsement, Mr. Stout. Major Ford is well thought of."

"Yes, Sir. He's a real good man. I was proud to ride with him."

"So how may I help you today?"

"Well, Cap'n, Sam here is ridin' a horse and saddle that I reckon belonged to this man." I handed him the wanted poster. "He is an orphan boy who met up with this Red, and his bunch, out on the plains. Sam didn't know they was outlaws 'til they robbed some folks, and he took no part in the robbery."

"So, how did Sam wind up with the outlaw's horse?"

Well, I explained to the Captain all about what had happened, even took him outside to show him the horse and saddle. I told him the folks we helped was here in the fort, since we had escorted 'em on in with us, and how I promised to get Sam a letter about how he come to have that horse, in case it was stolen.

"That will assuredly not be a problem, Mister Stout." And he proceeded to sit right down and write it out on official Army paper. Sam was mighty pleased to have it, 'cause it give him clear ownership to the horse and saddle unless a previous owner showed up. In that case, the letter would keep him from bein' hung as a horse thief.

"And how do you wish the reward to be paid, Mister Stout?"

I had not expected that, so I had to give it some thought. "You mean the army can pay it, just on our word?"

"Your word, the letter from Major Ford, the word of the Longs, and the evidence of the horse and saddle. That seems plenty to me, Sir. And, yes, the purser is authorized to pay it out, on my say so."

"Well dang," I said, "I reckon the four of us should share it. Can it be paid in gold, or must it be in paper?"

He laughed, "I'll authorize two hundred in gold, the rest in paper. How does that sound?"

"Real good, Captain. The boys will be plenty surprised at this. We didn't do it for no reward, but it'll be well received."

"That's exactly why it is my pleasure to pay it, Sir. Oh, and the Fort Commander would like to speak with you before you leave us. Take this chit to the purser's office and you will be paid. The sergeant will show you the way."

He handed me another piece of paper and went back behind his desk. I took that to mean we was dismissed, so I told him, "I appreciate your courtesy, Sir, and I'm sure the men will as well." We took our leave.

The sergeant pointed out the purser's office to us, and bid us a good day. As soon as he was back inside, Sam commenced to tellin' me how he couldn't take none of the reward money. He'd heard me say, "... the four of us," and he swore he didn't deserve none of it since he'd been with them owlhoots, and not with us.

"Sam, you weren't really with 'em," I told him. "You had a gun on your saddle, but never tried to use it. Had you been with 'em, you'd have joined in the fight. By not joinin' in, you helped us, so you get a share. Besides, you'll likely need it to get you settled somewhere."

"I don't know what to say, Mister Stout."

"Then don't say nothin'. Just put yore money somewhere safe, stay away from drink and gamblin', and you'll be okay."

"Can I stay with you and the others? I'd like to ride with you if I can."

We had talked some about what me and Bud and Leaping Deer was doin' out on the plains, and Sam thought he could help us. I figured he'd be better off with the Longs, since they had offered to take him in, and they seemed to be honest, decent folks.

"I'd be proud to have you, Sam," I told him, "But the Longs really need you more. They could use a strong man like you in helpin' 'em settle out west, and you'd be a great help to them. If you ever hear of me again, look me up. It's been a real pleasure knowin' you."

He looked down and toed the dirt at his feet before lookin' up at me and grinnin'. "I reckon yore right. I took a real likin' to them kids, and Missus Long's cookin' is mighty good. Guess I'll hook up with them, like you say."

After settlin' up with the purser, and givin' Sam his share, we headed down by the river to find the Longs' camp, and my friends. It seems the people they was to meet had already been here a couple of days, and they had set up next to them. I was introduced all around.

We had a last good supper with those folks, and I knew I'd met some fine people. These was the kind of people who would settle this country; farmers from Indiana, storekeepers from Pennsylvania, and other good people lookin' for a place to call their own, followin' a dream to their own destiny.

All they asked was a chance, the opportunity to carve something lasting out of a wilderness, and leave a legacy for them that come after 'em. It made me wonder at my own future. What lay in store for me and Mourning Dove? I say the both of us 'cause I was sure now that I'd find her somehow and, if I lived through it, we'd be back together again.

Finally takin' our leave, me and the boys moved down to where they had staked out a spot for our camp. On the morrow, we'd again head southwest from here, back into the Great Plains. I could be wrong, but somethin' told me Mourning Dove was within my reach. If so, we'd soon find her, and neither hell nor high water would keep me from her when we did.

~ ~ ~ ~ ~

After meetin' with the fort Commander the next morning—who just wanted to thank me and the boys for helpin' rid the area of outlaws—we spent a little time over coffee, discussin' our next move.

"Boys, for tradin', we have the two horses we got from the bandits, and that's about it," I was saying. "I need to buy some trade goods here at the sutler's, or the store in town. What do ya'll recommend?"

"I heard the Cheyenne like steel knives and pretty ribbons and such," Bud frowned, "But I shore don't know what we'd need to trade for the girls."

"I reckon I'll just go in and see what catches my eye. Maybe some cookin' pots for their women, along with some knives and trinkets. Now, here's my plan."

I proceeded to tell them how I thought we should head west by southwest, and then cut back to the southeast if we didn't hear somethin' first.

"That's where the Cheyenne like to camp, from what I hear. They stay south of the Oregon Trail while they're down here huntin' buffalo."

"So," says Leaping Deer, "We get trade goods, then we go."

The stores had a great variety of things that we thought the Cheyenne would like, but we had no real idea for sure. Nobody around here had traded much with them, 'cause the Cheyenne were getting' pretty hostile about all of the travelers going into their country. They were as likely to take your scalp as trade with you if they caught you unprepared.

I did like we had discussed, just bought a little bit of a bunch of things. Some would be real attractive to the women, and others would tempt the men. We'd have to hope it was enough, 'cause they weren't interested in gold or paper money. They thought white folks were crazy to trade for somethin' like that.

Once our packs were made up and loaded, we headed out in the direction of the far mountains. There was hundreds of miles of plains before we could even see those mountains, but we didn't plan to go that far. The idea was to go this way for about a week, cut more to the south, then head back toward the southeast, makin' a long U shaped swing through the heart of the plains. If we hadn't found the camp we wanted by then, we'd keep to the direction we was headed and go back into Pine Ridge to restock. After that, we'd go right back out, but cut straight across the area we had ridden around the first time. Surely, we'd find them then—if they were out there. Of course, even the best of plans can get changed.

We were three days out from the fort when Leaping Deer rode back to tell us he had spotted another camp ahead. Once again, I decked myself out in my finery, braided Buck's tail and mane, and headed for the camp. We'd decided I would do this one alone.

Just about the time I knew they had spotted me, I whistled at Rip and motioned my arm in a circle. He knew what to do from there, and took off to swing in a wide circle around the camp, stayin' out of range of anybody with a mind to harm him. They would only get glimpses of him now and then.

As always, I rode straight and tall in the saddle, lookin' neither left nor right as I rode into the center of the camp and pulled up before the biggest tee-pee there. Sittin' there admirin' the artwork on the tee-pee, my back felt itchy. Usually, somebody met me when I rode in and I never fretted about gettin' attacked. This time was different and I was beginnin' to think I had made a big mistake 'cause several bucks began to gather behind me and they didn't sound friendly.

I'd about decided to set the spurs to Buck and try to beat it out from there when the flap opened in front of me and a young-lookin' brave stepped out. He, too, was dressed in his finery and I figured that's what had taken him so long to come out.

He made a sight, he did. Standin' tall and proud before me, he indicated for me to get down off my horse. I did so, and hailed him, "Ya-ta-hay, my friend. I am Jonathon, friend of all people."

He looked like some kind of real leader standin' there. Around his neck was a beaded necklace with his medicine bag on it, and he wore a finely beaded rawhide shirt and pants. His long hair was not braided, but hung down past his shoulders and shone in the sunlight.

Dark, brooding eyes looked fully into mine without blinking, and he finally said, "I am called Satanta. The whites call me White Bear, a chief of the Kiowa."

His English surprised me, but I was proud he spoke it. It made communication a lot easier.

"I too am sometimes called by other names," I responded, "but my friends call me Jonathon. I would hope to be a friend to Satanta and his people."

"We shall see. Come, sit by my fire and we talk." With that, he opened the flap and stepped in before me, showin' his superiority. I shore didn't mind, it was his home, after all.

After we was seated cross legged by the fire pit, he asked me, "Why do you come to my camp? What do you seek here?"

"I have heard you are a friend to the whites, and that you may help me in my quest."

"My people have tried to be friends for a long time, but your people keep pushing us off our lands, killing our buffalo, and not honoring the treaties we have made. Maybe not friends much longer."

"I understand, Satanta, and I wish the bad whites were not among us, but I cannot change them or the things they do."

"If they do not change, maybe we will have to change them ourselves. We hoped for peace, to be allowed to hunt and live as we have always done. Why do your people not leave us alone to do this?"

"That I cannot answer, my friend, I can only speak of what is in my heart, not the hearts of others."

"So, Jonathon, why have you come?"

"Chief, I seek only to know where my wife might be, and her friend. They are of the Choctaw people and it is said they are with a band of Cheyenne, but I have yet to find them. My trail has been long, but I must stay on it until I find her."

"And then what will you do? Do you wish to kill those who took her?"

"No. I have found those who took her, and it was not the Cheyenne. The ones I found have told me where she may be.

That is why I look for the Cheyenne camp. I wish only to trade for her and her friend."

He sat quietly for a minute, just lookin' into my eyes. Finally he spoke again, "Why did you not say you are also called Spirit Warrior? Did you wish to deceive me?"

"No, my friend, you are too wise to be fooled. That is a name others would have me wear, not one I choose. I come in peace, not as a warrior, but a friend."

"Yet you come dressed as one of the people. Why do you wish to do so?"

"My wife is of the Choctaw. Her family took me in and saved my life. When we married, I became as one of them."

"Um," he grunted, and continued to look me over. Finally, I could wait no longer.

"Does the great Satanta or his people know of the woman of Jonathon? I ask only for knowledge of them, nothing more."

I didn't think he was gonna answer, then he suddenly spoke, "Yes, Jonathon, I know of them. Nearly a full moon ago, we met a band of the Cheyenne people moving to the east. With them, they had two young women who were not of their tribe, but carried bundles on their backs like slaves.

"I spoke with their leader about where they would hunt, so we would not go to the same place. He told me, and now I tell you."

I sat up straighter, and there's no doubt the interest showed in my eyes as he continued, "Go from here toward the Texas country. Do not enter the land of the Comanche but, after two days travel, turn back to the rising sun and you should find their camp soon after."

This was close to the way we had planned, but we likely would have missed them on our leg to the southeast, since we were planning to go further south of where he said.

"I thank you, my friend. Satanta is truly a good man."

"Maybe you can speak to the other whites, Jonathon. Tell them we wish to live in peace, but my young men are getting angry. Tell them to honor their words, and the ways of my people, so we may remain friends."

"I will speak to those I meet, and will tell them the words of Satanta, friend of the whites. I fear, though, that I cannot stop those who would dishonor themselves. I will try."

"That is all a man can do. I think you are an honorable man, Jonathon. I will remember you. Let the name of Satanta give you safe passage in our land. Maybe we will meet again."

"I hope so, my friend, I will also remember you. Thank you for your help. With the spirits to guide me, I will find what I seek and my heart will smile again."

Knowin' I had just met a great leader, I rode slowly out of the camp, thinkin' again of how close we were to findin' my bride.

Chapter 15

BUD AND LEAPING DEER was both excited to learn about the location of the camp. I tried not to get too excited until we actually saw the girls, 'cause it would be just too hard if this turned out to be different girls. Still, my hands were sweaty and my heart seemed to skip a beat now and again as we talked about it. This was our best chance yet, and I prayed it was the right one. It had been so long since I'd held her in my arms the ache was terrible. She had to be okay.

I could never again face the possibility she would not be found. If need be, the rest of my life would be spent in the far western mountains searching for her. I knew I couldn't ask my friends to spend their lives looking, but I could—and would—devote mine to that task. I could not face waking up as an old man and wondering if I might have found her in the next village.

It was only natural for us to want to rush off on the trail right away. As hard as it was, I knew we'd need to eat and sleep 'cause it might be more than a few days before we found the right camp, if at all. We stayed that night in the camp they had already set up for us, but I don't know if any of us slept. I didn't. The next mornin', after our usual little rodeo, we headed south.

The mornin' of the third day, skirting the edge of Comanche country, we turned east, toward the rising sun. We could pass within a few miles of the camp and never know it, but these was the directions Satanta had given me, so we hoped for the best.

Leaping Deer was out scouting every day. He rode twice as far as Bud and me did, but never seemed to tire. Me and Bud split up and rode about a half mile apart, each aware of where the other was, and within distance to head back real quick or to hear a gun shot. Towards evenin' of that day, Leaping Deer come ridin' back to meet me.

"Jon," he says, "I have seen sign of several unshod ponies, and found where someone has killed game. Tomorrow, I may be able to follow the trail to their camp. I do not know if it is the right one, we can only wait and see."

"Yes, we can only wait." I was so tired of waiting. The only thing in my life that mattered more than life itself was lost to me. My heart was weary, along with my body. It's not that I'm a particularly religious type, even though Paw taught me the bible, but I had been sayin' many a prayer lately. I just hoped He was listenin'.

Even though I tried not to be too hopeful, the next mornin', after another nearly sleepless night, I dressed in my white buckskins. We talked it over, and Bud rode with us on the trail, but would wait outside the village while me and Leaping Deer went in. The idea was that Leaping Deer, bein' from a friendly tribe, might give us more leeway in dealin' with the Cheyenne. I didn't mind goin' in by myself, but just thought it might pay off to have company this time. Besides, I didn't know any of the language and Leaping Deer was better at sign language.

It only took us a little while to find the spot where they had killed and cleaned their game the day before. From there, we sorted out the tracks and followed them northeast. We were back in country where I felt more comfortable, with some trees and small hills.

"Jon, look there." Leaping Deer's words snapped me out of bein' deep in thought. Holdin' up our horses, we looked out of the wooded area we was in to see a party of four bucks, mounted on some real nice horses, headed our way.

Seeing how they looked, bare-chested, wearin' only loincloths and tall moccasins, Leaping Deer declared, "Cheyenne, but not painted for war."

We knew this was a huntin' party, but didn't know whether to talk to them or keep ridin' for their camp. "What do you think?" I asked Leaping Deer.

"Maybe we go deeper into woods, let them pass, then you and I go to camp. Maybe they not happy to see us here."

Without another word, we eased our mounts deeper into the woods. About a quarter mile in, we stopped and talked it over.

"Bud, why don't you wait for us here? If we ain't back by dark, make your way back to our last camp, and we'll find you tomorrow."

"I can do that, Jon, but I'd feel better just stayin' here in these woods and not movin' around too much," he replied.

"Yep, I see what you mean. Okay then, we'll come back here when we leave the camp, no matter what. If we ain't back by tomorrow night, you'd best be thinkin' of getting' yourself back to Pine Ridge."

"You'll be back." He sounded more sure than I felt. I had no knowledge of the Cheyenne 'cept to know they was another tribe that was getting' plumb sore at the white folks.

It was a hard thing; the folks back east was wantin' somethin' to call their own, and the Indians was wantin' to hold on to their way of life. It seemed that the two was just not compatible.

By the time me and Leaping Deer had got back to where we first saw the hunters, they had passed by and kept on southward. We started on their back trail.

It was only a few more miles to the camp. We sat our horses and looked it over before goin' in. This was a fairly big camp, numberin' about forty teepees, and was spread over a good area. Women were busy scrapin' buffalo hides and smokin' meat, while kids roamed about the camp, playing.

Takin' a deep breath to settle my nerves, I nodded at Leaping Deer and we moved out. It wasn't but a minute before we was spotted, and the camp dogs set up a ruckus. People stopped what they was doin', some ducked into their teepees, to come out armed, while others just stood still and watched us come.

This was one of the biggest hunting camps I'd been in, and it took us a minute to figure out where to go. Leaping

Deer looked around and headed for the dead center of the camp, knowin' this was where the leaders probably were.

The Cheyenne were a good lookin' people, like the Comanche. I'd seen only a couple of the Apache, and they wasn't near as attractive. The women were mostly fairly tall, and slender, with pretty faces; the men were tall and sleek, well muscled, and fine specimens of manhood.

As we drew close to the center of the camp, we could see three braves waitin' for us. They were all tall, wearin' loincloths and leggin's, beads and medicine bags hangin' on their bare chests. Each wore feathers in his hair, but one had several eagle feathers and I figured him for the top dog.

Haltin' our animals, with the packhorse and spare mounts on leads, we waited for them to invite us down. A man never wants to just act like he has a right to be in a Indian's camp, but should wait for them to speak first.

"Ya ta hay." The one with the eagle feathers spoke first, and we replied in kind.

He then began to sign so fast that I lost it. Leaping Deer understood it, though, and began to dismount, so I followed his lead. Once we was on the ground, he started signin' some more, and Leaping Deer answered the same way, then told me, "He welcomes us to his camp, and asks why we are here."

"Tell him the truth," I said, "and tell him we have come ready to trade with him and his people."

Another exchange took place, some of which I understood. Leaping Deer then told me, "There are two Choctaw women here, but he says they are not his to trade."

"Ask if we can see them, and ask him who can trade for them."

After a minute, Leaping Deer said, "One of the girls belongs to the man here on our left. He is called Lame Elk. He may be willing to trade, but I asked to see her first."

That brave spoke rapidly to a woman nearby and she hustled away. Meantime, we kept discussin' the other girl. The leader insisted she was not his property, and we would have to deal with her owner.

"Aiieee!" We heard from behind us, and turned around to see Little Fawn running toward us. She cried out again, then threw herself into Leaping Deer's arms and wailed. He just held her close, and tried to calm her. An exchange in Choctaw revealed that Mourning Dove was also here. My heart leaped for joy, but my face never showed what I felt. At last! I had finally found her! I was determined to take her home, no matter the cost.

Turning back to the leader, I once again had Leaping Deer ask about Mourning Dove. A quick exchange revealed that the brave who owned her did not want to part with her.

"Tell him that she is my wife," I said, "and I must have her back, so that my lodge is no longer cold and empty. I ask to speak with this man who would keep my woman from me. To do so is not the way of honorable men."

Hearing my words, the chief looked thoughtful. Finally, shocking me, he asked in English, "Are you the one called Spirit Warrior?"

"Yes, I have been called that, but I did not ask for that name."

"You have been on this trail for two summers," he replied, "You must truly want this woman."

"Yes, my Cheyenne brother, and I will stay on it for many summers if need be. She is the one who warms my lodge and my spirit. I will do what I must do to see her home again. She belongs with her people, as does this young one."

"I will speak with the man who has her. Leave my camp and return alone, after the sun is high. We will see then."

"It will be done." We mounted up and rode out of camp, takin' our horses with us, leavin' a tearful Little Fawn behind. She knew, I hoped, that we would be back for her. Before we had gone a mile, I had to stop and get down from Buck. I was shakin' so hard that I was afraid he would get spooked. When my feet touched the ground, my knees gave way and I had to hold on to the saddle horn to keep from fallin'.

It took me a bit to calm down, but I was finally able to talk. "What happens now?" I asked Leaping Deer.

147

"You must do as he asked, and go back alone. I think the one man will trade for Little Fawn, but I don't know about Mourning Dove."

"You know I can't leave her here, not as long as I live."

"I know, Jon, but you may have to challenge the man's right to her. If you make it a personal challenge, he will have to fight you for her, or lose honor."

"How do I do that?"

"You must tell him he has no right to her, that your spirits are joined, and she belongs to you before all others. Offer to trade, but if he will not trade then you must say that one of you must die, because the Great Spirit would not wish for her heart to be torn between two men."

"And if he accepts my challenge?"

"Then you must kill him, or face death yourself. I will wait for you nearby, where I can watch the trail, but if you do not return by dark, then I will go to Bud and give him the news.

"After, I will return to the camp and bargain for Little Fawn. Then I will learn of your fate."

"I reckon it will have to happen," I said. "My hope is that he will trade after I make my pitch. If not, then we'll fight. There's no way I could steal her from a camp that size, and I'm sure she'll be watched real close now that they know we're nearby."

We sat down to wait, but I could not eat.

~ ~ ~ ~ ~

Shortly after the sun reached its peak, I rode back into the Cheyenne camp. The same tall, handsome warrior waited for me, but there were others by his side. I pulled Buck to a halt before them and dismounted. In English and sign, we talked.

"So you return, Spirit Warrior," he said. "I have spoken with the man who owns the woman, and he wishes her for his lodge. He will not trade."

"I offer respect and honor to the great Cheyenne people," I told him, "but I will not leave here again without my woman. I would challenge the man to fight with me for the right to her. The Great Spirit has told me it must be so."

He studied me closely for a minute, and then spoke again, "So you know of the Great Spirit and he speaks to you? Does he tell you that you may die in this quest?"

"I died the day she was taken. That is why I am called Spirit Warrior, because I am not of the living or the dead. I would die again if need be. Call this man; tell him I have come for her and I will not be denied."

"And what of the demon wolf who comes with you?"

"If I do not leave here with the woman, he will not linger. He will return to her family and tell them of the end of our journey. I have asked him to do so."

I had been noticing a tall, muscular brave of about twenty years listening closely to our talk. When I told how the demon wolf would not bother them, he seemed relieved. I figured he was the one I wanted, and I was proven right.

The chief motioned toward him and told me, "This is the man who would have the woman we speak of. He is called Red Fox. He paid a great price to buy her from the Shawnee, and wants her for his own."

"And what does the woman say?" I asked. "Does she wish to be his?"

"It is no matter. He paid for her, so he decides."

"No, the Great One decides. I have challenged him. Does he fear me? Will he accept the challenge, or will he lose his honor?" I got a little hot with this one, 'cause I wanted to settle this now.

"I will pay him these two horses and much more in trade. If he will not trade, then we must fight."

The chief looked at the brave in question. Red Fox stared at me for a minute and shucked off his buckskin shirt, pullin' a knife from his waistband. "I will fight the white man," he said, "He is no warrior."

"I rode with the one called Ford at the battle of the Canadian, against Iron Shirt's Comanche warriors, and I sang my death song on the day I started this quest," I told him. "I have no fear of it now. Let us begin." The chief translated what I said, and that got his attention.

The crowd that had gathered began to move back, makin' a sort of circle around us. There was a sudden disturbance when somebody shouted out somethin' in Cheyenne and pointed behind me. Lookin' that way, I saw Rip, closer than he had ever come to a camp, standin' and starin' at us. He lifted his nose to the sky and let out a howl worthy of any wolf.

Many in the crowd seemed shaken by that, and took to mumblin' amongst themselves, but I took no notice. I pulled the Bowie knife I had got in Texas and motioned the brave forward. For the first time, he looked really unsure. I reckon Rip, the Bowie, and my eagerness threw him off.

He knew how to handle a knife, and I saw right off that this would be a real battle. His knife was held loose in his right hand, point up, as he began to circle to his right. I matched him, move for move. A few feints from both of us kinda laid out the plan. We seemed to be pretty evenly matched in size and ability, so I had to find a way to surprise him, if I could.

Steppin' forward with his left foot, he leaned his body quickly towards me, and then leaped back as I cut the air where he had been. Just as quick as a snake, he reversed his direction and leaped forward again, bringin' his knife around in a swipin' motion. I felt the bite of his blade just under my left arm. He had drawn first blood. It was not a deep cut, but this was getting' serious.

Thinkin' hard about the hours spent with Paw, and all the things he had showed me, I tried to come up with a move. Meantime, Red Fox tried, again, to draw me in. This time I was ready for him and didn't bite. We kept circlin' to our right, each lookin' for an opening. He switched direction on me right quick, shifted his knife to his left hand, and moved left instead of right. This left him a shot at my right side, and he took it. I lowered my arm to protect my ribs, and again I felt the slice of his blade as it opened up a gash on my right shoulder.

For the first time, I began to worry. Already, he had cut me twice and I had yet to touch him. No matter how tough you think you are, the feel of cold steel slicing into your flesh will make you weak. Would this end in my death?

About then, I remembered a trick that Paw had used on me several times—until I got wise to it. I feinted toward his chest with my blade and, when he drew back, I slid to the ground with my feet tanglin' up around his. Usin' a scissor move, left leg low, right leg high, I kicked hard behind his knee, tripped him up, and threw him to the ground—hard.

He hit with a solid 'whump' and, ignoring my blood and pain, I was on top of him before he could catch his breath. While he was still shook up, I gripped his wrist and twisted it while beating his hand on the ground. His knife flew away. Then, I threw my weight onto his stomach, gripped him around the neck with my left hand, and put my blade tight against his throat. He froze where he was; to move was to die.

I knew I could kill him and nobody here would fault me, but I had no wish to see him die. I leaned close to his ear and said real low, "I will give you one horse and two of these big knives for the woman. Do you wish to trade with Spirit Warrior?"

At first I thought he would rather die, but the light left his eyes and he relaxed onto the ground. "It is more than I paid, so I will make a good trade. She is a hard woman, anyway."

To save his honor, I held him there, my knife drawing a thin line of blood from his throat. I raised my face to the sky and chanted a short song in Choctaw, then eased up from his prone body.

Lookin' around at the chief, I said, "The spirits tell me this man is a brave warrior. He has many hunts ahead of him, and many wives to care for before he dies. As they have said to me, let it be so; I will not take his life. If he will accept one horse and two of these great knives, we will trade."

The brave sat up. "The spirits have spoken, so it will be done. The Spirit Warrior is a wise and honorable man."

Stickin' my Bowie knife back in the sheath, I turned to the brave and stuck out my hand. Takin' it in his, he said, "We trade, the woman is yours."

He looked around at a young woman who had come close during the fight and told her something I didn't understand. She hustled away.

The horses was still standin' where I had left 'em, so we stepped over and he commenced to lookin' them over. He had a preference for the bay, the better horse, and raised his eyebrows at me. I nodded my head and he took up the reins. Then, I untied one side of the pack and reached in, pullin' out a package with four Bowie type knives in it. They wasn't the real thing, but kind of cheap replicas that didn't hold an edge like they should. They looked real, though, so he was right happy to get two of them.

I spotted the man who said he'd trade for Little Fawn and offered him the other two, and then pointed at the last of the outlaw's horses. He kind of motioned at the pack, so I knew he wanted more. Reachin' inside again, I felt around for the other package I knew they would like. It held red and blue ribbon, a couple of small mirrors, and a sack full of glass beads of all colors. Wantin' to keep things even, I give some of each thing to both men, and they were happy. I knew they would make some women happy, too. The chief looked real pleased at my actions. He had witnessed a good fight, had not lost a warrior, and was even more tickled when I gave him a mirror and some beads for himself.

There was a sudden commotion behind some of the folks gathered around. When I looked that way, I saw Mourning Dove forcin' her way through the crowd as fast as she could. The sight of her made my heart leap and, had we not been in this camp, I swear I would have cried from sheer joy and relief. It was really her!

I stepped in that direction and opened my arms wide. She finally broke through and just leaped into them, throwing her arms around my back and squeezing the life near out of me. She couldn't talk from weeping so hard. When I pulled her close to me and put my head down against her cheek, I looked right into the eyes of a small child, strapped into a carrier on her back.

Shocked ain't really the word to tell what I felt right then. I just held on to her and looked at that small, calm face, dark eyes just starin' back at me—so close I could smell the sweet breath of a recently fed baby.

"Oh, Jon, Jon. I was so afraid you would never find us." She finally whispered into my ear. "I love you so much."

Gatherin' my thoughts, and rememberin' where we were, I said, "And I love you, my Angel," then pulled slightly away from her so I could speak to the chief, even though I hated to let go.

"Where is the other woman, my brother? I will take her back to her family, too."

Before he could answer, Little Fawn came runnin' up to us and, laughin' while tears streamed down her cheeks, told Mourning Dove, "Jon has bought me, also. I get to go home with you."

They threw their arms around each other and the weepin' started again. I knew we'd likely never get out of here if this didn't stop.

Realizin' I didn't have enough horses left, I took the rest of the pack off of the roan and offered the pots and two iron skillets that was inside to the chief for two blankets. He accepted that trade, and I put both blankets across the roan's back and helped the girls mount. Because of packin' the baby, Mourning Dove got up behind Little Fawn. The girls had finally got hold of their emotions, and was quiet as we rode out of the camp—until we were clear.

Then, they both started talkin' up a storm, gigglin' one minute and cryin' the next. It was amazing to watch; they was so excited they couldn't stop. I didn't say anything 'til they calmed down a mite.

"Leaping Deer waits for us nearby," I told them, "and a friend is camped a little farther away, also waiting. They will be very happy to see you."

"What of my grandfather?" Mourning Dove asked me. "Is he well? I have worried about him."

"He was fine a short time ago. He was worried about you, also, and has kept our cabin clean, waiting your return."

"Oh, Jon, my heart nearly burst when I was told you had come to the camp. Red Fox left two women to keep me in the teepee so I could not come to you. They had to hold me back when another woman came to say you were going to fight Red Fox for me. I was so afraid."

"I know, honey. It's all over now and we're together again, where we belong."

"She said it was a death fight, but I saw Red Fox there before I could get to you. I almost died then."

"I could have killed him; I chose not to."

"Thank you, Jon. He was never mean to me, and his young wife was a friend. It would have hurt her to lose him."

"You didn't wed him?"

"No, Silly. I love only you." Catching my glance at her back, she laughed, "Oh, in all the excitement I forgot to introduce you to Grayson Little Bear Stout, your son."

I almost fell off my horse! My son? My son! Oh my God, I had a son! Then it hit me that she had to be expecting a baby when she was captured, before she even knew it herself.

My jaw dropped and I couldn't say a word.

I jerked on the reins, causin' Buck to slide a bit and throw his head up, then I slid down from his back and ran over to her. Pullin' her off of the roan, I held her close against me before flippin' back the bit of blanket she had covered his face with, and looked down again at the face of my own son. I was no longer the last of my line, and it pleased me, a lot, that she had named him Grayson, after my paw. I had come in search of my wife; I would return with my family. I gave silent thanks as my lips finally met hers, and I tasted the sweetness of my beautiful bride.

Leaping Deer was crazy excited when I rode in with both girls. He whooped for joy and hugged each of them for a long time. After lookin' at me and seein' a huge grin, he teased my son's nose with his fingertip and chuckled out loud.

"His name is Grayson Little Bear Stout," I proudly told him, "and he is our son."

"Waugh," he cried, "it is a good name. He will be a great warrior, like his father."

"I hope he never has to be a warrior, but if he does, I will teach him well, as my father taught me. And you can teach him to hunt, just as I taught you."

This brought a big laugh from everybody, and we all hugged again. Mourning Dove insisted on washing and wrapping my cuts before she would move from there, so I let her have her way. Then, we went to find Bud. On the way there, I told Mourning Dove a little about my good friend, and she spoke a bit about her servitude with the Cheyenne. The rest would wait for later.

Leaping Deer and Little Fawn rode a ways behind us, to give us privacy, and I could hear them chattering away. I knew he would want to hear all about the fight later, but I didn't want to talk of it for a while.

Urging our horses on, hoping not to meet the hunting party returnin' to their camp, we soon entered the woods where we'd left Bud. Buck sounded off as we got close, and Bud's horse answered from deep in a thicket.

We rode on into the clearing, and Bud stepped from behind a tree about thirty yards away, with a big grin on his face. "By golly! I just knew you'd find 'em. Let me meet the girl what has you so twisted up; she's gotta' be a doozy!"

Mourning Dove was now ridin' behind me, and she looked him over, nodded in approval, and slid to the ground beside Buck. "I am pleased to meet you, Mister Bud. Jon has told me of your friendship."

"Mister Bud? Now who would that be? My name is just plain ol' Bud, and that's what you gotta call me. Especially considerin' you are the wife of my best friend, and pretty as a Tennessee sunrise, to boot."

About this time, Grayson Little Bear made his presence known, the first sound he'd made other than a quiet chuckle when Leaping Deer teased him. Removing the pack and unstrapping him, Mourning Dove reached for the small pack she had stuffed in there with him. Taking it out and getting my canteen from the horse, she stepped away from us to fix his problem.

Bud gave me a queer look, but my face told him everything. "Aw naw, yore a daddy," he chortled, "Now how great is that? Jon, my boy, I envy you right now."

"Well, the way Tina talked about you, you might be one pretty soon, if you can stand up long enough to get hitched, that is."

He blushed beet red. "Now, dang it, you hadn't ought to be sayin' that. You might spoil my chances."

On the trail home, we all had a great reunion, sharing stories and catching up on everything. I even got to hold my son and play with him in the dirt. Bud whittled him a little bear from a piece of soft pine, and he loved to hold it when he rode with us.

By golly, I figured it would never be any better than this. My Angel was with me, I had good friends, and a son to watch grow into a man. Life was good again.

Chapter 16

IT DIDN'T TAKE US LONG to get back to our village. We knowed Owl Feather was desperate for any word of Mourning Dove, so Leaping Deer rode on ahead to give everybody the news. We had to travel a bit slower because of the girls and the baby, but all of us was in a hurry to get home. Bud rode along with us, and was his usual happy-go-lucky self, but there was times I saw him lookin' off into the distance and studyin' hard on somethin'. I had an idea what it was.

Before we even made it to the village, about a half dozen of the braves come ridin' out to meet us, whoopin' and hollerin' to beat all. The girls faces lit up like you wouldn't believe, and their eyes glowed like stars. Everybody wore big grins, and was talkin' so fast it was hard to understand 'em.

Owl Feather stood alone by his cabin when we rode in, tryin' to keep the stoic look of an elder on his face. When he saw Mourning Dove, it was too much for him, though. He broke into a grin that spread from ear to ear, showin' all the teeth he had left. She jumped from her pony and ran into the old man's arms, almost takin' him down. Grabbin' him around the neck, she hugged him 'til he was havin' trouble gettin' his breath.

"*Amafo!*" She cried, "I have missed you so much!"

"And I missed you, Granddaughter," he said, "So very much. My heart was afraid for you."

"Oh Grandfather, it was so frightening. Red Fox would not sell me, so Jonathon had to fight him for me. It was to be a death fight, and I was so afraid. Then Jon beat him but would not kill him, and he let me go. And Jon bought Little Fawn, too, and . . ."

"Whoa, Honey, slow down," I said, "There's time for all of that. Right now, just hug him close for awhile and introduce him to his great-grandson."

157

Her already sparkling eyes seemed to light up even more, and she slipped the papoose pack from her back, dropping it to the ground as she held onto the baby.

"Your great-grandson, Grayson Little Bear Stout," she proudly proclaimed as she held him out to Owl Feather. The old man beamed again, and took Grayson into his arms. The baby just looked up at him and smiled. All of the excitement and yellin' and all hadn't bothered him a bit. He just took it all in stride without even a whimper. That boy was some little man; it was hard to get anything but a smile from him. I reckon you could say I was proud.

We had a wonderful homecomin'. The whole tribe threw a big party for the girls that night, and Leaping Deer entertained them with some pretty wild stories about our exploits, even tellin' them that hadn't heard it about the Spirit Warrior and his demon wolf. They made me out to be some kinda hero, and it embarrassed me a lot, but I grinned and took it, even though I wanted to choke Leaping Deer. Then, of course, Bud had to tell it all again, his way. All in all, it was great fun.

Owl Feather had kept our cabin clean, and that night Mourning Dove made a bed for Grayson as I watched her. My heart seemed about to bust with joy while she puttered around, hummin' the same tune to him that I recalled hearin' when I lay near death on the ground. She soon got him settled in and turned towards me with a smile as bright as the full August moon.

"Oh, Jon, I am so happy. We are together again, with our son, and my spirit is filled with love and joy."

"Mine also, my love, mine also."

She came over and snuggled in next to me, holding me tight. This was the best day of my life, and I was complete again. I said a silent, "Thank You," to the one that made it possible.

After breakfast the next mornin', we all was sittin' and talkin' about the happenings of the past year or so. Bud kept scratchin' and shiftin' around like somethin' was bitin' at him, and I finally just told him, "Bud, don't you think you ought to go back to Pine Ridge and let Sarge and them know how it turned out?"

"Well, I reckon I could, but I hate to run out on ya'll so soon."

"Naw, that's fine. We got lots of catchin' up to do, so it'd be nice if somebody let 'em know." I knew he was chompin' at the bit to get back there, but he'd never admit it.

"If your shore you won't need me, I reckon they are kind'a worried."

"Now, Bud, if you don't want to go, then you know you're welcome to stay with us. I don't mean to run you off or nothin'. On second thought, why don't you just stay here, we can send one of the young'uns to let them know." Now I was pokin' him a little, just for fun.

"No, no. You was right the first time. I know Sarge and Lawassa was worried somthin' terrible about you and Mournin' Dove. It's only right that I go spare them any more grief."

"Well, okay, if you think that's best."

He like to have knocked over several people on his way to saddle up. I couldn't keep from grinnin' at the way he tore outta' there. Mourning Dove was looking at me with a question in her eyes, so I explained about Christina.

"We need to get over and see tham before too long," I told her. "They was sure enough worried about you."

"Of course, Jon. I learned quickly to love them and to see how much they care for you. We will go soon."

~ ~ ~ ~ ~

The next couple of weeks we spent renewing old friendships among the people of the village. As word spread, people came from miles around to see us, hug Mourning Dove and Little Fawn, and make a big deal over Grayson. Of course, he was a special baby, so I kinda expected that.

When we could get off alone, or in the quiet of the evenin', me and Mourning Dove talked of everything. We had so much to catch up on. She told me more of life with the

Cheyenne, and I told her of the vast reaches of Texas. I didn't say too much about our battle with the Comanche, but she gave me one of her looks when I skimmed over it, like she understood it weren't a proud time for me.

When I spoke of Texas, the wide open spaces and land there for the takin', she took to studyin' me real closely. I talked of how a man could make a real future for his family there, and how I wanted more for her and Grayson than to live on the reservation all their lives.

One day she surprised me with, "Jon, why don't we all go to Texas?"

"Huh?"

"I mean it. You sound so full of life when you speak of it, and I can see it is in your heart to go somewhere where you, I, and our little one can have a different life, so let's go."

"But, Honey, I never really expected you to leave here. I love it here, and the people are the best. This is your home."

"I know you love it, but your heart cries out for more. One thing I learned while away from you is that my home is wherever you and our son are. That is what makes me happy, not a place. I have spoken with Grandfather, and he will go with us, or stay, whichever you wish. He loves us all, and he understands how a man feels about making a better life for his family."

"Gosh, Honey, I hadn't really give it a lot of thought. I reckon I was just sharin' my dreams with you. Are you sure it'd be alright?"

"Did I not say so? Now, let us talk of it further."

"Well, I reckon it won't hurt to discuss it. And, if we go, Owl Feather definitely goes with us, if he wants to."

"His heart is as mine, Jon. His home is with you, me, and our son. Remember, his first home was back east, and even though he has lived here many years, he will gladly go with us."

"Hmmm, I guess we oughta be thinkin' on it then."

Chapter 17

WE SPENT A LOT OF TIME talkin' over our future after that. I had quite a bit of money, what with my Ranger pay and the reward money we'd collected, so I could get us a wagon and mule team. I knew, too, that if I wrote to Major Ford, he'd make sure we got land just about wherever we wanted to settle.

My dream was to build a ranch for my family, stock it, and watch it grow. I'd have to hire somebody who knew cattle, 'cause I sure didn't, but we could manage that for a while. Once we sold the first cattle, we'd be able to pay up.

So, me and my darlin' wife set down to talk it over with Owl Feather after we made our decision. I run it all past him, but he weren't no cattleman either, so I couldn't pick his brain on that matter. He was, however, a very wise man, and he pointed out a couple of things I'd missed. Anyway, with my family in agreement, except for Grayson—and he voted with his pa—we went to work on our plans.

First off, I hunted for enough meat to last us awhile. Owl Feather and Mourning Dove set about smokin' meat and makin' pemmican for the trail while I went to Fort Smith to buy a wagon and some mules. By the time I got back, they had everything sorted out that we was gonna take with us, and had food packed up and ready to load. There was some mighty tearful good-byes, and we offered to take Little Fawn with us, but she wanted to stay with her family, as did Leaping Deer. We knew we might never see these fine folks again, and even I got a bit teary eyed at the idea. We kept it together with the knowledge that our future lay before us, and it could be a grand one.

~ ~ ~ ~ ~

It hadn't been easy gettin' the loaded wagon out from the village. There weren't really a road goin' in there, but more of a trail. With the four good Missouri mules, and by cuttin' down a coupla small trees, we made it through to the road.

Owl Feather mostly drove the wagon, with Mourning Dove and Grayson on the seat beside him, while I rode Buck. By afternoon, I could tell he was getting' tired so I took over the reins and Mourning Dove would move to the back, just behind the seat.

That big old freight wagon, with a canvas cover, had enough room for sleepin' space for all of us. In good weather, me and Mourning Dove would likely sleep underneath, leavin' the bed to the oldest and the youngest. Once he was fed and tucked in, Grayson slept through the night with no problem. He was about the happiest, and easiest goin' baby I ever saw. Mourning Dove was a wonderful mother, and had done a bang-up job with him. I prayed I could be half as good a pa to him.

By the time we wheeled into Pine Ridge, we had a regular routine goin'. It would stand us in good stead for the long trip ahead. I pulled the wagon up close beside the store, and helped the family get down just as Sarge and Lawassa appeared on the porch.

"Mourning Dove," Lawassa cried, "Come, come, let me hug you. Oh, and I must hold that beautiful baby; Bud has told us so much." I was invisible right now, as it should be.

But Sarge couldn't get to them, so he grabbed me. "Jon, I'm so proud of you, Boy. It does my old heart good to see the two—no, make that three—of you together. We had been sittin' on pins and needles 'til Bud rode in. It's so good to see ya'll."

Laughin', I hugged him back and we beat on each other's backs for a while. "Speakin' of Bud, where is he? I need to talk to him."

"Oh, him and Tina rode out again today. They're spendin' near every day together, and I hear weddin' bells in the air." Sarge grinned even bigger.

"Well, it couldn't happen to a better man. Him and Tina make a real nice couple. How do Dave and Sandy feel about it?"

"They're tickled pink. There ain't many good men to be found around here, and they're right pleased to see Bud and Tina so happy. Say, Jon," he continued, "What's with the wagon? Ya'll movin' out from here?"

"Yessir, we're goin' to Texas to try and build a ranch. I was hopin' Bud would go along, but I reckon there's another voice to be heard from now. Here, let me introduce you to Owl Feather."

I made the introductions, and the oldsters hit it off right from the start. I knew they would, since they was both smart men, and had lived the same rough life.

Sarge and Lawassa shooed us all into the cabin and insisted on feedin' us. I wasn't gonna complain, it might be the last time I'd get to eat Lawassa's cookin', and I'd sure miss it. Mourning Dove was a great cook, but Lawassa was a genius in the kitchen. Somehow, she made the same old foods take on a new flavor. And, like I knew they would, they both made a big fuss over Grayson. That boy just naturally made everybody around him happy. 'Course, I was a tiny bit biased, I reckon.

Late that afternoon, Bud and Tina rode in. They'd been out ridin' in the hills and talkin', like me and Mourning Dove had done. Anybody with an eye could see how much they adored each other, and I heard the same bells that Sarge did.

After the usual fuss over us, the huggin', cryin', and talkin', I took Bud aside. "What are your plans, Partner?" I asked him. "You and Tina talkin' about a future?"

"Dang right we are," he beamed. "Soon as we can find a preacher, we're tyin' the knot, and I hear there's one down at Fort Towson right now."

"I thought you was scared of getting' hitched."

"Not to Tina I ain't. Jon, she's the best thing I ever hoped to find. She done stole my head and my heart. I swear the sunrise comes from that woman's eyes."

"I know the feelin'," I laughed, "It pleases me to no end to hear about it. Ya'll are made for each other."

"Pard, I saw the wagon but never got around to askin' about it. What's goin' on?"

"Me, Mourning Dove, our son, and Owl Feather are headin' to Texas. We want to start and build a ranch, if we can. I thought to ask you to join us, but now you have Tina to consider."

"Well Friend, we done talked about it. She loves her uncle Dave and aunt Sandy, but she knows there ain't much future here. Dave has the smithy, Sarge has the store, and, except for some crops and a few cattle, nobody else has much. Besides, this is the Choctaw's land and these folks are allowed what they have by the good graces of the tribe."

"I see. So what do you think about Southwest Texas? There's plenty of room, plenty of stray cattle, and we could build a good ranch there if we can avoid the Apache and the Mexican bandits."

"Well, we hadn't settled on a place yet, but that sounds good to me. I'll run it by Tina and see what she thinks, but I reckon she'll go wherever I want to go. Meantime, I'll get somebody to ride down to Fort Towson for the preacher. I cain't wait to get in double harness with that gal." His face said it all.

Of course we decided to wait around for Bud and Tina's wedding. Me and Mourning Dove asked them if we could stand up beside 'em, since we'd never had a Christian wedding, and she kinda wanted one. I was happy with what we had, but her church schoolin' made her want to get married again, in the Christian way. Whatever she wanted was fine with me, and they said they was proud to stand with us.

The kid who Bud had sent to find the preacher came back with good news, and Bud give him a whole two dollars, makin' him swell with pride. The preacher was comin' the next day, so the girls spent all of that day makin' weddin' plans while me and Bud had a couple of drinks and talked of our plans.

First, we was gonna' build a cabin separated by a dog run. There'd be a big room to each side, one with a fireplace, and a open space between 'em, all under one roof, and we'd share it. Later, we'd pick a spot and build another cabin just like it for Bud and Tina, about a mile away. His ranch would spread to the south from midway between the cabins, ours would spread to the north. There ain't many folks I would plan somethin' like that with, but I knew me and Bud could make it work.

The next mornin', as the sun was risin' into a clear blue sky, we all got married. For us it was the second time, but it made Mourning Dove happy, and she looked more lovely than ever. We had agreed to put Tina's things in our wagon while Bud trailed the roan and another packhorse Dave had give them for a weddin' present. Neither of them had enough to need a wagon, so it worked out fine.

There was more tearful, but joyous, good-byes when we made ready to head out. Sarge pumped my hand and said, "I know you'll go far, Jon. You're a special man, and they don't come along often. Just watch your back, take care of your family, and send us a letter now and then."

"I will, Sarge. I'm gonna miss all of ya'll up here. You have all been so good to me. It's been a hard row at times, but friends like you have made it easier."

"Well," he said, as a tear slid down his creased old cheek, "I recollect the orphan boy what showed up at my door a while back. Now, I see the man I knowed he could become. God bless you all, my boy, and Texas better git ready for ya', 'cause you'll make it yores."

With those words in my ears, I mounted up and led the wagon out of the clearing. Texas, here we come.

Author's Bio

Roger Haley was born and raised in Northeast Texas. He was brought up helping his father and brothers haul hay, cut, stack, and deliver firewood, pick cotton, or whatever else needed doing.

He is a life member of the Veterans of Foreign Wars, a member of the American Military Retiree's Association, and a Vietnam veteran. After retiring from the US Navy, Roger returned to the place he called home, to be near his extended family. He started and managed a variety of businesses in the intervening years, including a small trucking company, and a family construction company still in business. During his trucking years, he finally made it to Vermont, the last on his bucket list of the 50 states he had wanted to visit.

Semi-retired now, he devotes his time to writing. He is a regular contributor to local newspapers, a freelance article writer, and works on his books.

Roger is also a member of Western Writers of America, and attended his first conference in Knoxville, Tennessee, in 2010 where he finally met some of his idols.

Today, he and his wife, Georgia, still live in the country near the Red River, in Northeast Texas. You're welcome to contact him at www.rogerhaley.com and leave comments or questions in his guest book. He tries to respond to all messages left for him.

RAMBLE HOUSE's

HARRY STEPHEN KEELER WEBWORK MYSTERIES

(RH) indicates the title is available ONLY in the RAMBLE HOUSE edition

The Ace of Spades Murder
The Affair of the Bottled Deuce (RH)
The Amazing Web
The Barking Clock
Behind That Mask
The Book with the Orange Leaves
The Bottle with the Green Wax Seal
The Box from Japan
The Case of the Canny Killer
The Case of the Crazy Corpse (RH)
The Case of the Flying Hands (RH)
The Case of the Ivory Arrow
The Case of the Jeweled Ragpicker
The Case of the Lavender Gripsack
The Case of the Mysterious Moll
The Case of the 16 Beans
The Case of the Transparent Nude (RH)
The Case of the Transposed Legs
The Case of the Two-Headed Idiot (RH)
The Case of the Two Strange Ladies
The Circus Stealers (RH)
Cleopatra's Tears
A Copy of Beowulf (RH)
The Crimson Cube (RH)
The Face of the Man From Saturn
Find the Clock
The Five Silver Buddhas
The 4th King
The Gallows Waits, My Lord! (RH)
The Green Jade Hand
Finger! Finger!
Hangman's Nights (RH)
I, Chameleon (RH)
I Killed Lincoln at 10:13! (RH)
The Iron Ring
The Man Who Changed His Skin (RH)
The Man with the Crimson Box
The Man with the Magic Eardrums
The Man with the Wooden Spectacles
The Marceau Case
The Matilda Hunter Murder
The Monocled Monster

The Murder of London Lew
The Murdered Mathematician
The Mysterious Card (RH)
The Mysterious Ivory Ball of Wong Shing Li (RH)
The Mystery of the Fiddling Cracksman
The Peacock Fan
The Photo of Lady X (RH)
The Portrait of Jirjohn Cobb
Report on Vanessa Hewstone (RH)
Riddle of the Travelling Skull
Riddle of the Wooden Parrakeet (RH)
The Scarlet Mummy (RH)
The Search for X-Y-Z
The Sharkskin Book
Sing Sing Nights
The Six From Nowhere (RH)
The Skull of the Waltzing Clown
The Spectacles of Mr. Cagliostro
Stand By—London Calling!
The Steeltown Strangler
The Stolen Gravestone (RH)
Strange Journey (RH)
The Strange Will
The Straw Hat Murders (RH)
The Street of 1000 Eyes (RH)
Thieves' Nights
Three Novellos (RH)
The Tiger Snake
The Trap (RH)
Vagabond Nights (Defrauded Yeggman)
Vagabond Nights 2 (10 Hours)
The Vanishing Gold Truck
The Voice of the Seven Sparrows
The Washington Square Enigma
When Thief Meets Thief
The White Circle (RH)
The Wonderful Scheme of Mr. Christopher Thorne
X. Jones—of Scotland Yard
Y. Cheung, Business Detective

Keeler Related Works

A To Izzard: A Harry Stephen Keeler Companion by Fender Tucker — Articles and stories about Harry, by Harry, and in his style. Included is a compleat bibliography.

Wild About Harry: Reviews of Keeler Novels — Edited by Richard Polt & Fender Tucker — 22 reviews of works by Harry Stephen Keeler from *Keeler News.* A perfect introduction to the author.

The Keeler Keyhole Collection: Annotated newsletter rants from Harry Stephen Keeler, edited by Francis M. Nevins. Over 400 pages of incredibly personal Keeleriana.

Fakealoo — Pastiches of the style of Harry Stephen Keeler by selected demented members of the HSK Society. Updated every year with the new winner.

Strands of the Web: Short Stories of Harry Stephen Keeler — Edited and Introduced by Fred Cleaver

RAMBLE HOUSE's OTHER LOONS

Alexander Laing Novels — *The Motives of Nicholas Holtz* and *Dr. Scarlett*, stories of medical mayhem and intrigue from the 30s.

Amorous Intrigues & Adventures of Aaron Burr, The — by Anonymous — Hot historical action.

Angel in the Street, An — Modern hardboiled noir by Peter Genovese.

Anthony Boucher Chronicles, The — edited by Francis M. Nevins Book reviews by Anthony Boucher written for the *San Francisco Chronicle*, 1942 – 1947. Essential and fascinating reading.

Automaton — Brilliant treatise on robotics: 1928-style! By H. Stafford Hatfield

Best of 10-Story Book, The — edited by Chris Mikul, over 35 stories from the literary magazine Harry Stephen Keeler edited.

Black Dark Murders, The — Vintage 50s college murder yarn by Milt Ozaki, writing as Robert O. Saber.

Black Hogan Strikes Again — Australia's Peter Renwick pens a tale of the outback.

Black River Falls — Suspense from the master, Ed Gorman

Blood in a Snap — The *Finnegan's Wake* of the 21st century, by Jim Weiler

Blood Moon — The first of the Robert Payne series by Ed Gorman

Case of the Little Green Men, The — Mack Reynolds wrote this love song to sci-fi fans back in 1951 and it's now back in print.

Case of the Withered Hand, The — 1936 potboiler by John G. Brandon

Charlie Chaplin Murder Mystery, The — Movie hijinks by Wes D. Gehring

Chelsea Quinn Yarbro Novels featuring Charlie Moon — *Ogilvie, Tallant and Moon, Music When the Sweet Voice Dies, Poisonous Fruit* and *Dead Mice*

Chinese Jar Mystery, The — Murder in the manor by John Stephen Strange, 1934

Clear Path to Cross, A — Sharon Knowles short mystery stories by Ed Lynskey

Compleat Calhoon, The — All of Fender Tucker's works: Includes *Totah Six-Pack, Weed, Women and Song* and *Tales from the Tower*, plus a CD of all of his songs.

Compleat Ova Hamlet, The — Parodies of SF authors by Richard A. Lupoff — A brand new edition with more stories and more illustrations by Trina Robbins.

Contested Earth and Other SF Stories, The — A never-before published space opera and seven short stories by Jim Harmon.

Cornucopia of Crime, A — Memoirs and Summations of 30 years in the crime fiction game by Francis M. Nevins

Crimson Clown Novels — By Johnston McCulley, author of the Zorro novels, *The Crimson Clown* and *The Crimson Clown Again*.

Crimson Query, The — A supervillain from the 20s by Arlton Eadie.

Dago Red — 22 tales of dark suspense by Bill Pronzini

Dancing Tuatara Press Books — *Beast or Man?* by Sean M'Guire; *The Whistling Ancestors* by Richard E. Goddard; *The Shadow on the House, Sorcerer's Chessmen, The Wizard of Berner's Abbey, The Ghost of Gaston Revere*, and *Master of Souls* by Mark Hansom, *The Trail of the Cloven Hoof* by Arlton Eadie and *The Border Line* by Walter S. Masterman, and *Reunion in Hell* by John H. Knox, and *The Tongueless Horror* by Wyatt Blassingame. With introductions by John Pelan. Many more to come!

David Hume Novels — *Corpses Never Argue, Cemetery First Stop, Make Way for the Mourners, Eternity Here I Come*, and more to come.

Day Keene Short Stories — League of the Grateful Dead, We Are the Dead and *Death March of the Dancing Dolls*. Collections from the pulps by a master writer. Introductions by John Pelan.

Dead Man Talks Too Much — Hollywood boozer by Weed Dickenson

Death Leaves No Card — One of the most unusual murdered-in-the-tub mysteries you'll ever read. By Miles Burton.

Deep Space and other Stories — A collection of SF gems by Richard A. Lupoff

Detective Duff Unravels It — Episodic mysteries by Harvey O'Higgins

Devil Drives, The — A prison and lost treasure novel by Virgil Markham

Devil's Mistress, The — Scottish gothic tale by J. W. Brodie-Innes.

Dime Novels: Ramble House's 10-Cent Books — *Knife in the Dark* by Robert Leslie Bellem, *Hot Lead* and *Song of Death* by Ed Earl Repp, *A Hashish House in New York* by H.H. Kane, and five more.

Don Diablo: Book of a Lost Film — Two-volume treatment of a western by Paul Landres, with diagrams. Intro by Francis M. Nevins

Dope Tales #1 — Two dope-riddled classics; *Dope Runners* by Gerald Grantham and *Death Takes the Joystick* by Phillip Condé.

Dope Tales #2 — Two more narco-classics; *The Invisible Hand* by Rex Dark and *The Smokers of Hashish* by Norman Berrow.

Dope Tales #3 — Two enchanting novels of opium by the master, Sax Rohmer. *Dope* and *The Yellow Claw*.

Dr. Odin — Douglas Newton's 1933 potboiler comes back to life.

Dumpling, The — Political murder from 1907 by Coulson Kernahan

Edmund Snell Novels — *The Sign of the Scorpion, The White Owl* and *Dope and Swastikas* (*The Dope Dealer* and *The Crimson Swastika*)

End of It All and Other Stories — Ed Gorman's latest short story collection

Evidence in Blue — 1938 mystery by E. Charles Vivian

Fatal Accident — Murder by automobile, a 1936 mystery by Cecil M. Wills

Finger-prints Never Lie — A 1939 classic detective novel by John G. Brandon

Freaks and Fantasies — Eerie tales by Tod Robbins, collaborator of Tod Browning on the film FREAKS.

Gadsby — A lipogram (a novel without the letter E). Ernest Vincent Wright's last work, published in 1939 right before his death.

Gelett Burgess Novels — *The Master of Mysteries, The White Cat, Two O'Clock Courage, Ladies in Boxes, Find the Woman, The Heart Line, The Picaroons* and *Lady Mechante*

Geronimo — S. M. Barrett's 1905 autobiography of a noble American.

Gold Star Line, The — Seaboard adventure from L.T. Reade and Robert Eustace.

Golden Dagger, The — 1951 Scotland Yard yarn by E. R. Punshon

Hake Talbot Novels — *Rim of the Pit, The Hangman's Handyman.* Classic locked room mysteries.

Hell Fire and **Savage Highway** — Two new hard-boiled novels by Jack Moskovitz, who developed his style writing sleaze back in the 70s. No one writes like Jack.

Hollywood Dreams — A novel of the Depression by Richard O'Brien

House of the Vampire, The — 1907 poetic thriller by George S. Viereck.

I Stole $16,000,000 — A true story by cracksman Herbert E. Wilson.

Inclination to Murder — 1966 thriller by New Zealand's Harriet Hunter

Incredible Adventures of Rowland Hern, The — 1928 impossible crimes by Nicholas Olde.

Invaders from the Dark — Classic werewolf tale from Greye La Spina.

Jack Mann Novels — Strange murder in the English countryside. *Gees' First Case, Nightmare Farm, Grey Shapes, The Ninth Life, The Glass Too Many.*

Jim Harmon Double Novels — *Vixen Hollow/Celluloid Scandal, The Man Who Made Maniacs/Silent Siren, Ape Rape/Wanton Witch, Sex Burns Like Fire/Twist Session, Sudden Lust/Passion Strip, Sin Unlimited/Harlot Master, Twilight Girls/Sex Institution.* Written in the early 60s.

Joel Townsley Rogers Novels — By the author of *The Red Right Hand: Once In a Red Moon, Lady With the Dice, The Stopped Clock, Never Leave My Bed*

Joel Townsley Rogers Story Collections — *Night of Horror* and *Killing Time*

Joseph Shallit Novels — *The Case of the Billion Dollar Body, Lady Don't Die on My Doorstep, Kiss the Killer, Yell Bloody Murder, Take Your Last Look.* One of America's best 50's authors.

Jvlivs Caesar Mvrder Case, The — A classic 1935 re-telling of the assassination by Wallace Irwin that's much more fun than the Shakespeare version

Keller Memento — 500 pages of short stories by David H. Keller.

Killer's Caress — Cary Moran's 1936 hardboiled thriller

Koky Comics, The — A collection of all of the 1978-1981 Sunday and daily comic strips by Richard O'Brien and Mort Gerberg, in two volumes.

Lady of the Terraces, The — 1925 adventure by E. Charles Vivian.

Lord of Terror, The — 1925 mystery with master-criminal, Fantômas.

Marblehead: A Novel of H.P. Lovecraft — A long-lost masterpiece from Richard A. Lupoff. Published for the first time!

Max Afford Novels — *Owl of Darkness, Death's Mannikins, Blood on His Hands, The Dead Are Blind, The Sheep and the Wolves, Sinners in Paradise* and *Two Locked Room Mysteries and a Ripping Yarn* by one of Australia's finest novelists.

Muddled Mind: Complete Works of Ed Wood, Jr. — David Hayes and Hayden Davis deconstruct the life and works of a mad genius.

Murder in Black and White — 1931 classic tennis whodunit by Evelyn Elder

Murder in Shawnee — Novels of the Alleghenies by John Douglas: *Shawnee Alley Fire* and *Haunts.*

Murder in Silk — A 1937 Yellow Peril novel of the silk trade by Ralph Trevor

My Deadly Angel — 1955 Cold War drama by John Chelton

My First Time: The One Experience You Never Forget — Michael Birchwood — 64 true first-person narratives of how they lost it.

Mysterious Martin, the Master of Murder — Two versions of a strange 1912 novel by Tod Robbins about a man who writes books that can kill.

N. R. De Mexico Novels — Robert Bragg presents *Marijuana Girl, Madman on a Drum, Private Chauffeur* in one volume.

Night Remembers, The — A 1991 Jack Walsh mystery from Ed Gorman

Norman Berrow Novels — *The Bishop's Sword, Ghost House, Don't Go Out After Dark, Claws of the Cougar, The Smokers of Hashish, The Secret Dancer, Don't Jump Mr. Boland!, The Footprints of Satan, Fingers for Ransom, The Three Tiers of Fantasy, The Spaniard's Thumb, The Eleventh Plague, Words Have Wings, One Thrilling Night, The Lady's in Danger, It Howls at Night, The Terror in the Fog, Oil Under the Window, Murder in the Melody, The Singing Room*

Old Times' Sake — Short stories by James Reasoner from Mike Shayne Magazine

One After Snelling, The — Kickass modern noir from Richard O'Brien.

Organ Reader, The — A huge compilation of just about everything published in the 1971-1972 radical bay-area newspaper, THE ORGAN.

Poker Club, The — The short story, the novel and the screenplay of the seminal thriller by Ed Gorman

Private Journal & Diary of John H. Surratt, The — The memoirs of the man who conspired to assassinate President Lincoln.

Prose Bowl — Futuristic satire — Bill Pronzini & Barry N. Malzberg .

Red Light — History of legal prostitution in Shreveport Louisiana by Eric Brock. Includes wonderful photos of the houses and the ladies.

Researching American-Made Toy Soldiers — A 276-page collection of a lifetime of articles by toy soldier expert Richard O'Brien

Ripped from the Headlines! — The Jack the Ripper story as told in the newspaper articles in the *New York* and *London Times.*

Robert Randisi Novels — *No Exit to Brooklyn* and *The Dead of Brooklyn.* The first two Nick Delvecchio novels.

Roland Daniel Double: The Signal and The Return of Wu Fang — Classic thrillers from the 30s

Rough Cut & New, Improved Murder — Ed Gorman's first two novels

Ruled By Radio — 1925 futuristic novel by Robert L. Hadfield & Frank E. Farncombe

Rupert Penny Novels — *Policeman's Holiday, Policeman's Evidence, Lucky Policeman, Policeman in Armour, Sealed Room Murder, Sweet Poison, The Talkative Policeman, She had to Have Gas* and *Cut and Run* (by Martin Tanner.) This is the complete Rupert Penny library of novels.

Sam McCain Novels — Ed Gorman's terrific series includes *The Day the Music Died, Wake Up Little Susie*

Sand's Game — A selection of the best of Ennis Willie, including a complete novel.

Satan's Den Exposed — True crime in Truth or Consequences New Mexico — Award-winning journalism by the *Desert Journal.*

Secret Adventures of Sherlock Holmes, The — Three Sherlockian pastiches by the Brooklyn author/publisher, Gary Lovisi.

Sex Slave — Potboiler of lust in the days of Cleopatra — Dion Leclerq.

Shadows' Edge — Two early novels by Wade Wright: *Shadows Don't Bleed* and *The Sharp Edge.*

Shot Rang Out, A — Three decades of reviews from Jon Breen

Sideslip — 1968 SF masterpiece by Ted White and Dave Van Arnam

Singular Problem of the Stygian House-Boat, The — Two classic tales by John Kendrick Bangs about the denizens of Hades.

Slammer Days — Two full-length prison memoirs: *Men into Beasts* (1952) by George Sylvester Viereck and *Home Away From Home* (1962) by Jack Woodford

Smell of Smoke, A — 1951 English countryside thriller by Miles Burton

Snark Selection, A — Lewis Carroll's *The Hunting of the Snark* with two Snarkian chapters by Harry Stephen Keeler — Illustrated by Gavin L. O'Keefe.

Stakeout on Millennium Drive — Award-winning Indianapolis Noir — Ian Woollen.

Suzy — Another collection of comic strips from Richard O'Brien and Bob Vojtko

Tales of the Macabre and Ordinary — Modern twisted horror by Chris Mikul, author of the *Bizarrism* series.

Tenebrae — Ernest G. Henham's 1898 horror tale brought back.

Through the Looking Glass — Lewis Carroll wrote it; Gavin L. O'Keefe illustrated it.

Time Armada, The — Fox B. Holden's 1953 SF gem.

Tiresias — Psychotic modern horror novel by Jonathan M. Sweet.

Totah Six-Pack — Fender Tucker's six tales about Farmington in one sleek volume.

Triune Man, The — Mindscrambling science fiction from Richard A. Lupoff

Ultra-Boiled — 23 gut-wrenching tales by our Man in Brooklyn, Gary Lovisi. Yow!

Universal Holmes, The — Richard A. Lupoff's 2007 collection of five Holmesian pastiches and a recipe for giant rat stew.

Victims & Villains — Intriguing Sherlockiana from Derham Groves

Wade Wright Novels — *Echo of Fear, Death At Nostalgia Street* and *It Leads to Murder,* with more to come!

Walter S. Masterman Mysteries — *The Green Toad, The Flying Beast, The Yellow Mistletoe, The Wrong Verdict* and *The Perjured Alibi, The Border Line, The Curse of Cantire.* Fantastic impossible plots.

Werewolf vs the Vampire Woman, The — Hard to believe ultraviolence by either Arthur M. Scarm or Arthur M. Scram.

West Texas War and Other Western Stories — by Gary Lovisi

Whip Dodge: Manhunter — A modern western from the pen of Wesley Tallant

White Peril in the Far East, The — Sidney Lewis Gulick's 1905 indictment of the West and assurance that Japan would never attack the U.S.

You'll Die Laughing — Bruce Elliott's 1945 novel of murder at a practical joker's English countryside manor.

Young Man's Heart, A — A forgotten early classic by Cornell Woolrich

RAMBLE HOUSE

Fender Tucker, Prop.   Gavin L. O'Keefe, Graphics

www.ramblehouse.com   fender@ramblehouse.com

228-826-1783   10329 Sheephead Drive, Vancleave MS 39565

CPSIA information can be obtained at www.ICGtesting.com
Printed in the USA
LVOW13s2339301013

359308LV00002B/465/P